MURDER
AT THE
SPANIEL
SHOW

BY LYNN HALL

Flyaway
Letting Go
The Solitary
Danger Dog
Mrs. Portree's Pony
If Winter Comes
Just One Friend
Tazo and Me
The Something-Special Horse
The Giver
Uphill All the Way
The Boy in the Off-White Hat
Megan's Mare
Denison's Daughter
Half the Battle
Tin Can Tucker
Danza!
The Horse Trader
The Leaving

MURDER AT THE SPANIEL SHOW

LYNN HALL

CHARLES SCRIBNER'S SONS
NEW YORK

Copyright © 1988 by Lynn Hall

Charles Scribner's Sons Books for Young Readers
Macmillan Publishing Company
866 Third Avenue, New York, NY 10022
Collier Macmillan Canada, Inc.

Printed in the United States of America
First Edition   10 9 8 7 6 5 4 3 2 1

Library of Congress Cataloging-in-Publication Data
Hall, Lynn.   Murder at the spaniel show/by Lynn Hall.
—1st ed. p. cm.
Summary: Sixteen-year-old Tabby wonders what connection lies between her boss, a blind dog breeder, and the sinister death threats to his twin brother who has arrived to judge an important national show.
ISBN 0-684-18961-5
[1. Dog shows—Fiction. 2. Dogs—Fiction. 3. Blind—Fiction.
4. Physically handicapped—Fiction. 5. Twins—Fiction.
6. Mystery and detective stories.] I. Title.
PZ7.H1458Mu 1988 [Fic]—dc19   88-18244 CIP AC

MURDER
AT THE
SPANIEL
SHOW

Wednesday, June 26

·1·

My world was being invaded. Well, not exactly invaded, and not exactly my world. But Quintessence felt like my world, and even though I was excited about what was happening there, the vans and motor homes coming up our private road did feel a little bit like an invasion.

I don't actually live at Quintessence, although I'd love to. I work here, summers, and I have a little room of my own over the kennel. My family lives just four miles away, and of course I have to live there during the school year, at least for two more years till I get out of high school. Then, I'm hoping to move to Quintessence permanently and work for Mr. Quinn.

My name is—are you ready for this?—Tabby. I hate it. It's Tabitha, but what else are people going to call a Tab-

1

itha? I wouldn't mind Tabby so much if I looked like an alley cat, you know, lean and hungry and street-smart. Unfortunately I look like a Persian kitten, sort of round and soft. But that's just on the outside. In my mind I'm lean and hungry and street-smart, but nobody believes it.

If I weren't mentally lean and hungry, I'd never have landed a job with Turner Quinn. For two reasons. One, I'd never have gone looking for a job like this, and two, Turner Quinn doesn't suffer fools gladly. Everyone who works for him is mentally sharp, even down to his lowliest kennel girl, me. He likes it that way.

A year ago last spring I decided to go looking for a super kennel job. I'd always been a dog nut. Lots of my friends were horse nuts, and I like horses, too, but what really turns me on is a beautiful purebred dog, groomed to perfection and standing in perfect show pose. What I really love about show dogs is that when they break that perfect pose, they instantly turn into joyful, loving, game-playing, silly huggy-bears.

There are plenty of kennels in my area, which is right on the New York–Connecticut state line, not too far north of New York City. There are big, shabby boarding kennels, and little private show kennels, and hobby breeders with a few pens of scuzzy-looking dogs. But none of these was what I was after. I wanted to land in a place like Quintessence, so I kept asking around at veterinarians' offices and dog shows whenever I could get to one. And eventually it paid off.

I rode my bike—I wasn't driving yet—up the long, curvy, blacktop road north out of Katonah one day last spring, turned in through the brick gateposts by a small, expensive-looking sign saying QUINTESSENCE, and rode on up some more of the curvy blacktop road to the house. I found the kennel, found the kennel manager, and offered myself to her for the summer. She looked me over for a while, asked me several hundred questions, and finally took me to Mr. Quinn.

He was a surprise, at that meeting. He still is. The first thing I noticed about him was that he was blind. His eyes were unfocused and rolled upward, and when he stood to be introduced I could tell he was homing in on the sound of my voice. He held out his hand and left it to me to find it. I did.

He was around early fifties, I guessed, but lean and athletic looking. His hairline had receded halfway back on his head, but the black and gray hair that was left was expensively cut. He'd have been a very handsome man except for the funny halfway-back hairline and, of course, the wandering eyes.

"So you think you want to work in a kennel?" His voice was detached, as though his mind were on more important things. "What makes you think shoveling dog piles is going to be a wonderful way to spend the summer? You won't meet boys working in a show kennel, you know."

"If I wanted to meet boys I'd be applying at Pizza Hut," I snapped before I remembered to play it cool.

But he smiled a tiny smile, and I got the impression that he liked employees who spoke up to him.

"I want to work here," I said, "because show dogs are

3

what I plan to build my life around, and I want to do my learning at the best show kennel I can get into."

He zeroed in on me more intently. "And you think Quintessence is the best?"

I sucked in my breath and gambled on my instincts. "I don't have any real way of knowing which is the best show kennel around here. I picked out five that look good from the outside, and the first two I went to didn't need any summer help. You're the third."

He grinned at me then, and said, "Nancy, put her on the books. Do whatever you want with her. What'd you say your name was? Tabby? They name you after a cat, or what? What does she look like, Nancy?"

The kennel manager was a small, stringy-looking woman, late thirties, with ultrashort, tannish gray hair and hard little gray-green eyes. She looked me up and down, and said, "Medium height, a little overweight but clean and neat looking, dark brown hair, short and clean, no makeup." She squinted in for a closer look at my face. "Blue eyes, nice clear skin, round features. Pug nose. Looks cheerful and intelligent. Red oxford-cloth shirt, newish jeans, tennis shoes."

I felt like a fool standing there being described to him, but I could understand his wanting to know what his employees looked like. So I smiled at him even though he couldn't see the smile. Nancy would probably report it to him later, I figured.

The rest of that spring I worked weekends at the kennel, and as soon as school was out, I moved into the little room over the garage and became full time. I learned the dogs' names and quirks, which ones were on restricted diets, which ones could and could not be turned out together. I fed them, picked up feed pans and washed them, checked the automatic waterers in each run, wielded the pooper-scooper in the gravel runs and in the exercise yards, and helped Nancy with whatever she needed help with. I held puppies for their shots, I led mama dogs while Nancy led puppies, lead-breaking them. I bathed dogs just before their trips on show weekends, and learned to pin their towels around them to keep their coats lying flat while they dried.

The Quintessence dogs were springer spaniels, beautiful, powerful, midsize dogs with black or brown bodies, white legs and necks and face markings. There were several older dogs, retired champions, some international champions, most with obedience, tracking, and hunting test degrees after their names. Several were young adults currently working on their titles. A few were adolescents being grown out for future showing, and there was usually a litter or two of babies. I loved them all.

For a rich guy, Turner Quinn didn't have very many people working for him. Mr. and Mrs. Jasper lived in a former guest house; he did the lawn work and she did the housekeeping and cooking for Turner. Mr. Jasper also helped in the kennel when I wasn't there, but he was getting on in years, and he had an incredible amount of mowing to do. Nancy Polaski was the kennel manager and show handler. Then there was me, and that was it.

Of course the first thing I did when I started working there was to ask Nancy about Mr. Quinn. She called him

Turner. His father had built Quintessence, she told me, and Turner had grown up here. Back then it had been a nice place, a comfortable brick house built on the site of an old farmstead. Turner's father ran it as a hobby farm, but his main business was an accountancy firm in Katonah. The place didn't turn into an estate until later, when Turner made a bundle by inventing a few needed medical gadgets and starting a company to manufacture them. He started medical school but just couldn't keep up, because back then they didn't have all the learning aids they have now for visually disabled students. But he had a very quick, inventive mind and the ability to visualize problems and solve them. He came up with his first invention when he was still in college, an improved tip for rubber tubes used to pump stomachs.

He made a ton of money with his medical engineering firm, built wings onto the old square original house, turned the entire farm into lawns—if you can believe 180 acres of lawn—and got serious about the kennel. His father had bred springers for years, when Turner and his brother were growing up. So when he started getting rich, Turner built up the kennel into one of the top springer kennels in the country. Then, a few years before I came along, he retired from the engineering business to become a big shot in the Empire State Springer Spaniel Club, the White Plains Kennel Club, and the American Kennel Club.

At first my job was just in the kennel, but by the end of last summer I was spending half my time with Turner, helping him with office work or just keeping him company. He liked me. I liked him, when I wasn't scared of him. Most of the time he was okay, but when he was in one of his black moods, look out Nelly.

By this summer I had evolved into a sort of general assistant and gofer, especially since I got my driver's license. And not a moment too soon, as Turner liked to say, because this summer, this very weekend, Quintessence was to be the site of the eighty-ninth annual National English Springer Spaniel Specialty Show. The official host organization was the Empire State Springer Spaniel Club, of which Turner was currently president. Quintessence, with its 180-acre front yard, was an ideal show ground. Everyone was delighted about the whole thing, even I when I had time to be delighted.

Mostly I was dashing off in all directions at once.

·2·

I stood in the road with my right arm out, pointing. The approaching motor home slowed, hesitated, then followed my direction to the right, across the grass toward the broad, open area where the tents and rings would be set up tomorrow. The main house and kennel stood behind me, on a slight rise, shaded by lawn trees and shrubbery. The expanse to my right and downhill was a former hayfield rimmed by woods and lined with a beautiful curve of low stone wall.

To my left, on the other side of our private road, was a belt of woods following a pretty little stream. Beyond the

7

stream were more grassy fields where, today, a team of tracking judges were working. Beyond those fields and circling in back of the house were rougher fields with patches of second-growth trees and clumps of rock. Back there would be the hunting trials tomorrow.

The main show area on my right was already beginning to take on a necklace of motor homes parked in a loose circle along the stone wall, where the trees beyond the wall would make afternoon shade. Twice already that day I'd had to walk down there and ask people not to park in the center area where the rings would be set up later.

I'd just come back from taking a thermos of lemonade to the tracking judges in the field beyond the stream. They'd been designing and staking out tracks for two hours in the hot sun. I'd stayed and talked to them for a while, as they drank. I intended to use this show to learn as much as I could about everything I could.

The judges, who were a husband and wife team, explained what they were doing. Laying out twelve tracks, they said, one for each of the twelve dogs that was entered in tomorrow's tests. Each track was about five hundred yards long, and each turn in the track was marked by a red flag. As they laid out the tracks, they drew maps on their clipboards. Eighty yards from starting flags toward dead elm, right turn, one hundred yards to patch of dark green weeds, left turn, fifty yards toward small cedar tree . . . and so on. Tomorrow, at specified times, an official track-layer would walk the track, following the flags and the maps, leaving his scent on the grass and dropping a glove at the end. After a half hour, the dog assigned to that track would then have to follow the scent until he found the glove or got hopelessly lost and flunked the test.

I'd have liked to stay and watch, but duty called. After I directed the motor home into the camping area, I trotted up the hill toward the house to see what Turner wanted me to do next. I'd lost the mood I'd had earlier, of being invaded. That was just preshow tension, probably. I'd been running Turner's errands so frantically the past week that I'd had a little spell of nostalgia at the last minute for the calm and pleasant routine I was used to.

But now things were getting started, and I began to feel hostessy. Playing the lady of the manor, which was silly considering that I was the kennel girl. But it was fun, anyway.

When Turner built the kennel, he built it as a wing on the house. It was easier for him to navigate around the place if all the buildings were adjoined, he'd explained. The only separate buildings on the place were the guest house, out close to the road, where the Jaspers lived, and an old stable building out back, where the mowers and lawn tractor lived.

Adjoining the house was a three-stall garage, with my room up over it. Then the kennel was beyond the garage, with Nancy's apartment over it. The kennel was T-shaped, a huge, square workroom for grooming, mixing feed, and whelping puppies. The long part of the T was indoor-outdoor runs, comfortable minirooms indoors for each dog, with swinging doors leading to nice, clean gravel runs outside. I know they were nice, clean runs because I was the one who kept them that way.

Between the big, square workroom and the garage was the kennel office, which was one of my favorite places. It had comfortable easy chairs, a fireplace, and a big desk where I did lots of work, typing pedigrees and stuff like that. Of course there were trophies all over the place, and show-win photographs and a glassed cabinet full of the more important rosettes—the Best in Show and Group First rosettes. Nancy didn't bother to keep mere ribbons. She either used them for bookmarks or just threw them away.

The office was set up to be headquarters for the show, and I expected to find Turner in there, ordering things on the phone or typing up lists of things to check on. He was surprisingly accurate on the typewriter, and used it a lot.

There was a man standing beside the desk when I went in and, coming out of the sun's glare, I assumed it was Turner. The man was bent over the desk, poking through papers.

He straightened guiltily and turned to me. I didn't know him. He was a smallish man with a badly broken nose. It went east when he went north, it was so badly bent out of shape. He was neatly dressed, in sport slacks and a short-sleeved striped cotton shirt. Dark hair grew low on his forehead.

"Anybody from the show committee around?" he asked.

"Mrs. Abernathy was around here somewhere," I

said. "She's the show chairperson. Big woman, blond hair, lots of jewelry. I'd guess she's down by the rings somewhere. Or Turner should be around here someplace. Anything I can do for you?"

I could tell by the way he looked at me that he was one of those guys who puts kids and human beings in separate categories. Even if all he'd wanted was directions to the john he wouldn't have asked me. Okay by me if he wanted to be that way. I knew more about what was going on here than six Mrs. Abernathys in spite of all her fuss and feathers, but if he wanted to go chasing her down, that was fine with me.

He started out the door, collided with Turner, stumbled over Turner's cane, and went on across the lawn without bothering to apologize. Turner had his own way of handling people like that. His cane was the long, slim, white kind with an elastic cord down its hollow center so that it could be folded up to about eighteen inches long with a couple of snaps of the wrist, and unfolded to full length just as fast. Turner didn't use it much around the house and kennel because he knew his way and didn't need it. But it was amazing how often rude people, bumping into Turner, got their legs tangled in a white cane they hadn't known was there. Turner could snap that sucker out to full length and trip a person before you could blink.

"I'm here," I said.

"Oh, good, Tab. I was looking for you. Where's Nancy?"

"Last time I saw her she was out with the hunting test

11

judge, walking him around the fields back there. Want me to go chase her down?"

He looked annoyed, and folded his cane with three angry movements. He snapped open the cover of his braille watch and felt the time. "Almost three-thirty. The Quinns' plane gets in at five, didn't you say? You'd better go pick them up. They're coming into the White Plains airport. You can get there all right, can't you? And listen, take this typewriter back and pick up ours, and would you fill up the car and have them check the oil, and I want you to stop at the florist and check to be sure they've got the order right, judges' corsages and the arrangements for the ring tables. You've got the list somewhere, haven't you?"

"Right," I said, somewhat wearily. "Typewriter, car gas and oil, florist, airport. I'd better get going. I'm just wearing shorts. Is that okay for meeting judges, or should I change?"

"Make it a skirt, and get going."

"Yes, master," I muttered, but not until I was halfway up the stairs. That man could hear thoughts in your head. There was a little stairway from the kennel work-room up to a landing. From the landing, a left turn took you into Nancy's apartment, a right turn took you into my little room.

It was nice. Shaggy rugs, a dormer window with window seat under it, bed and dresser and my TV from home, a comfortable chair to dump clothes on, and a great big closet. And a teeny bathroom; can't forget that.

I grabbed a denim skirt, pulled off shorts, combed hair more or less, and grabbed my purse. Car gas and oil, typewriter, florist, airport. Clattering down the stairs, I grumbled silently. Some of these errands weren't all that necessary. Come on, Turner. Car gas, okay, check on floral arrangements, okay, but returning the loaner typewriter and picking up ours was not all that necessary on a day as busy as this. For that matter, sending our typewriter out to be cleaned two days ago was dumb, in my humble opinion.

But Turner could be like that. He was used to having people do things for him, and he didn't always stop to think that his demands might be a little unreasonable.

I jammed the florist list in my purse, unplugged the typewriter, and heaved it out the door and into my car.

Once I was on the road, I got over my bitchy mood. It was a terrific car to drive, a small but luxurious Cadillac Cimarron. I whipped through the errands in Katonah and headed down the highway toward the White Plains airport.

I was eager to get a look at the judge I was picking up. He was flying over from England with his wife to judge the Specialty Show.

His name was Ted Quinn, and he was Turner's twin brother.

Turner's twin, who was never mentioned at Quintessence until the show committee hired him to be the premier judge at the Specialty.

Turner's twin, whose name caused a tightening in the cords of Turner Quinn's neck.

·3·

I pulled up in front of the White Plains terminal and parked along the sidewalk by what looked like the main entrance. It was a shabby little airport, as airports go. I'd been here twice with Nancy, when she came to pick up a bitch being flown in from Texas for breeding and again a few days later when we shipped the bitch home again. But that was from the Air Express office. This was my first look at the passenger terminal.

I was such a whiz at errand-running that I had ten minutes to spare before the Quinns' flight was due to land. It was just a short connecting flight up from Kennedy International. I was hoping it might be late, so I'd have time to grab a sandwich or at least a bag of nacho-flavored corn chips. I live for nacho-flavored anything. And I'd been running hard since lunch. A can of diet soda and a handful of nice, salty nacho chips would have been ambrosia of the gods right then.

But, no luck. The plane coasted down out of the sky precisely on cue. I stood against the newspaper vending machine by the door and watched the line of people coming across the pavement from the small plane. I ignored the lone businessmen and stared only at the couples, watching for a man who looked like Turner.

There was only one couple the right age, and he didn't look very much like Turner, at least not at first glance. He was much heavier, for one thing. Stout body, double chin, puffs under his eyes. And his hair was so thick, so bright a brown, that it might as well have had RUG written across it in neon lights. Already I didn't like this man.

The wife was a turnoff, too. She was the kind of woman who automatically made me feel dumb, young, and clumsy. She was ten or fiften years younger than her husband. Her hair was aggressively auburn, like his hairpiece. Her lips were dark red and would have been nonexistent if she hadn't painted a pair of upward points under her nose. Her eye makeup was, shall we say, garish? Shall we say ridiculous?

They stopped a little distance from me and stood looking around, obviously expecting to be met, but not by a teenager. They looked right through me. For this I changed into a skirt?

"Mr. and Mrs. Quinn?" I went up to them and held out my hand, determined to impress them with my adult good manners. "I'm Tabby Trost, your brother's assistant."

Ted Quinn looked nonplussed for a second, as though I'd spoken in a foreign language, then he shook my hand as briefly as he could, and wiped his palm against his trouser leg. That really frosted me. My hands were clean and dry; he didn't need to do that. Louise Quinn gave me a stiff smile and a nod, the kind of nod that's meant to ward off a handshake.

We jammed their luggage into the Cimarron's trunk and took off. Louise shared the back seat with the newly cleaned typewriter, and Mister Personality got in front with me. I could tell he would rather have been in back, but I was damned if I was going to shift the typewriter just for him. He rode all the way home with one hand braced against the dash and a foot pumping imaginary brake pedals.

Looking in the rearview mirror, I asked Louise, "Is this your first trip to America?" Be polite. Make conversation.

"No, no, Ted does quite a bit of judging here," she said. "I always come with him."

"Oh." I'd have asked her how she liked it here, but I was afraid she'd tell me. She struck me as the sort who didn't like much of anything.

"Where are the judges staying?" Ted asked me.

"There at the house—at least you and the Tomases are." Sally Tomas was the other conformation judge who, along with Ted Quinn, would be judging on Saturday and Sunday. "The tracking judges have their own motor home, and the hunting, obedience, and puppy stakes judges live in the area, so there'll be just you two and the Tomases staying at the house."

Louise said under her breath, "I'm surprised he didn't put us up at the Budget Motel."

I opened my mouth to protest, then closed it again. Obviously there was no love wasted between Turner and Ted Quinn, for reasons I couldn't even guess, but surely they had expected to stay at Quintessence. Hadn't they? After all, it *was* Ted's family home.

Months ago, when we'd begun working on the plans for the Specialty Show, and when Ted Quinn was hired to judge Bitches and Best in Show, I'd asked Nancy about him.

Ted Quinn had gone into dogs after college even more seriously than Turner, she told me. He'd made several trips to Europe and England, buying promising show dogs for American clients. He was licensed to judge all the spaniel breeds, in America and in England, by the time he was thirty. He'd married a wealthy Devonshire breeder who was quite a bit older than he and who conveniently died a few years later, leaving him the estate in Devonshire and plenty of money to run it. Louise was Wife Number Two. Through the years Ted had added breeds to his list, and he was now licensed to judge all breeds in England, all sporting breeds in America, and several breeds in France and Germany. He was a popular judge with show-giving kennel clubs because he didn't charge very much. He seemed to feed on the ego-feast of being a judge, and he certainly didn't need the money.

I asked Nancy why Turner seemed to hate his brother's guts, but she had no idea. Ted had been long gone from the country when she came to work at Quintessence eighteen years ago, and any time she'd mentioned his name to Turner he'd bitten her nose off. Figuratively speaking, of course.

I was literally tingling with curiosity and anticipation as I drove through the gate and up our road. The fields beyond the brook were empty of people, but dotted with the track-layers' flags, awaiting tomorrow's competition. The field beyond the stone wall held several more motor homes and vans than when I left.

Ted and I carried their suitcases up the impressive, curved, brick steps toward the front door. There was a brick terrace here, raised above lawn level, with small trees in big pots lined up along the house. The door was a double one, with springer spaniel heads, in brass, for knockers.

I pushed the door open with my hip and led them into the air-conditioned hall. Turner emerged from the huge formal living room to the right of the hallway. I figured he was waiting for them in there, for the sake of the impression the room made. He didn't ordinarily use it.

Holding out his hand in the direction of our noises, he said, "Welcome, Ted, Louise." I noticed he didn't say welcome home.

Ted shook Turner's hand, then wiped the handshake off against his pant leg as he'd done with mine. Nothing personal, apparently. He must wipe off everybody like that, I thought. What a turkey. Louise evaded the hand-shake by nodding her head, then realized he couldn't see the nod, and reached to meet his hand just as he gave up on her and dropped it.

Turner said in his cool-but-cultivated voice, "Did you have a good flight over? Had no trouble finding my chauffeur, I take it." He held out his hand, open-fin-gered, toward me, and I stepped close so he could grasp my shoulder. We walked in that position a lot, out-doors.

They exchanged a few stilted sentences about the flight over from Heathrow, which I assumed was the London airport. Then Turner said, "Tab, take Louise and Ted up to the green room and see they've got everything they need, all right? Did you take care of the other errands?"

18

"Yep. Everything's under control. You want to come this way?" I said to the Quinns, then realized awkwardly that I was showing Ted around his own former house. Oh well, he wouldn't know which was the green room after all these years.

It was a large, pleasant bedroom at the front of the house, second only to Turner's own room across the hall. I set down my load of luggage, and made a gesture around the room.

"Bathroom is through that door over there, closets there, you can adjust the air conditioner to however you want it. It's that little knob on the front."

On the dresser was a spray of flowers I hadn't expected to see. The florist's card peeked out.

"How nice," Louise said, and pulled the card out of its envelope. "From the show commit—" She froze, staring at the unfolded square of paper in her hand.

"What is it?" Ted demanded. Travel-weary irritation sounded in his voice. Wordlessly Louise handed the paper to him.

He read it and was struck as dumbfounded as his wife. I looked over his shoulder and read it myself. It was neatly typed, and brief.

"Ted Quinn. If you judge Best in Show, you will be killed."

· 4 ·

"Someone's living my fantasy," Nancy said. "Murdering a judge."

19

"Nobody's been murdered yet, and nobody's going to be. It's just somebody's idea of a sick joke."

We were sitting on the floor of a puppy pen in the corner of the grooming room. Behind me in the main kennel all runs were scooped clean and hosed down, all feed bowls eaten empty and washed, all dogs settled in their beds for the night.

I'd just discovered a fact that the rest of the world probably already knew. In times of stress and upset, there was nothing as soothing as the familiar routine of chores that must be done. I think people who take care of animals have a kind of serenity, and this is where it comes from, the ordered, daily routine of chores. No matter if a crazed murderer may be on the loose at Quintessence, five o'clock is still feeding time.

It was close to seven by now. Nancy and I should have gone up to her apartment, where we shared our thrown-together meals, but she seemed reluctant to leave the dogs and I, too, found the big, bright grooming room a comforting place to be at the moment.

Seven brown-and-white puppies tumbled around our legs, making snarling attacks on our shoes and each other and trampling one another to climb into our laps. Nancy had nail trimmers and was laying one pup at a time against her upraised knees to nip off the sharply pointed puppy toenails.

I held a puppy, too, laying him on his back to tickle his chest and make wings out of his ears.

"So who are you guessing?" Nancy asked as she snipped a nail.

20

"What who?"

"Who are you guessing wrote the note? Boss man?"

"You've got to be kidding. Don't kid about a thing like that, even in private." I glanced around the room as though I expected listening ears.

"Come on," Nancy said, her leathery face pulled long, teasing me. "Don't try to tell me Turner wasn't the first name that popped into your head. This is not exactly the city of brotherly love here, you've noticed."

"Oh well, sure, but that's a long way from murder threats. I mean, I can't stand my brothers most of the time, but still . . ."

"So what are they doing about it?" She motioned with her head toward the house. She'd been showing puppies to a prospective buyer who was here for the show when I'd brought the Quinns from the airport, so she'd been getting the story from me in small bites while we worked.

"Well, they did finally call the Katonah police station and tell them about it, but I had the feeling nothing much was going to be done. Turner seems to think the whole thing is a joke. Old Ted was pretty shook up when he read it, though, and so was his wife. She's a rare bird. Lips up to her nose."

Nancy said dryly, "So is Teddy the Wonderjudge going to withdraw, or what? Did the note say he'd be killed if he judged Best in Show, or if he judged, period?"

"If he judged Best in Show." I said. "Who could want to get him off the judging assignment badly enough to stick a murder threat in his flowers? I mean, come on. If

21

you don't want to show under a judge, don't enter that show."

Nancy scowled and looked at me through the blade of her nail cutters, like Sherlock Holmes with his magnifying glass. "That would be true for an ordinary show, but don't forget, this is the National Specialty. All the top springers in the country will be here, plus some from Canada, England, Japan. Whoever wins Best in Show here this Sunday will be top dog in the breed for a year, like Miss Universe. It's the highest achievement a breeder or handler can shoot for. A once-in-a-lifetime thrill, and of course a small fortune in future stud fees and puppy sales."

I could tell from her voice that she was aching to be in the running this year. Last year, when the National was held in Salt Lake City, Nancy had flown out with two puppies, an Open Class bitch and a newly finished champion, Buddy, alias Champion Quintessence Quite-A-Guy. Buddy had been a two-year-old then, not quite mature enough to hope for Best in Show but even so, he'd been pulled out for final consideration from a class of sixty. This year he was at his peak. This year he would have been a genuine contender except that club rules forbade officers of the show-host club from competing. This was to prevent an influential member from pressing to hire a judge he knew would favor his dog, perhaps a judge who was a personal friend.

I scowled. "If they changed judges at the last minute, it wouldn't mean Buddy . . . no, of course not. Entries were closed two weeks ago."

Nancy shook her head. "No, Turner's dogs couldn't compete this year, no matter who was judging."

"So is there somebody entered who would benefit from a change in judges?" I asked, holding up my puppy and touching noses with him.

Nancy hummed a little as she thought. "Well, if Ted backed out of judging Best in Show but did the rest of his assignment, then probably what would happen would be that Sally Tomas would take over the Best in Show class. And sure, there are any number of people entered who would have a better chance under her than under Ted. Sally is a movement judge. If a dog's got an iffy shoulder assembly or a short stride or a soft topline when it gaits, Sally'd dump it.

"Ted Quinn, on the other hand, goes for the big coats, the lean heads, the dogs who look elegant when they're posed, even though they may fall apart when they gait. So, basically, people with sound, good-moving dogs would benefit by a switch to Sally, while people with elegant but less sound dogs would rather have Ted. But still, the specials that will be entered here are going to be the cream of the crop. Most of them will be dogs good enough to do well under either type of judge."

"And with competition like that," I mused, "nobody could be sure enough of winning to make it worthwhile to risk a stupid move like threatening the judge. I mean, you wouldn't do something like that unless you knew for a fact that the substitute judge would give you the win."

Nancy stood and stretched, and I followed her. "That's right, and I just can't imagine any dog-show exhibitor going to those lengths, even to win the National Specialty. I mean, that's unreal."

The puppies were already played out, and had curled up in pairs, throats crossed for warmth and security while they slept. I turned out the light and followed Nancy up the stairs in the corner of the grooming room. Neither of us felt like cooking much, which wasn't unusual. We kept stocks of Dinty Moore beef stew and chili and awful canned Mexican food for times like tonight, when running the can opener was about as much as we could handle.

I loved her apartment. In fact I dreamed of living in it. It was one long room under sloping roof angles, with big windows at the far end overlooking the dog runs and exercise yards. Like my room, it was carpeted in deep shag of a soft green, and furnished with bird's-eye maple. The kitchen was along one of the sloping walls, with a round maple table for our meals.

We were greeted by our mutual roommate, an ancient black-and-white bitch with bleary eyes and dreadful breath. Sadie was American and Canadian Champion Quintessence Sadie Thompson, UDT, the *UD* being an advanced-level obedience degree, the *T* denoting her tracking degree. She and Nancy were very close; Sadie had lived in the apartment for years. Nancy had fitted the apartment's doorknobs with rubber covers, so that Sadie could turn them with her mouth when she needed to go out in the night. One kennel run was left empty, so that when Sadie's weakening bladder demanded a night exit, the old dog could mouth open the apartment door, trot downstairs and through the kennel, go out the dog door in the run, and take care of things.

I figured Sadie was Nancy's main love in life. Nancy had chosen dogs over husband or children and had elected to care for someone else's dogs rather than her own. A boss like Turner, who gave her a free hand in the kennel, and a dog like Sadie, who was virtually Nancy's own, probably made up for a lot. In fact, I saw Nancy's life as completely enviable.

After supper I helped wash up our stew pan and two plates; then I took a can of diet soda from the fridge and went across the landing to my room. I knew Nancy well enough by now to know that she liked me, and tolerated my company during the day with good humor, but that she was a loner by nature and cherished her evenings alone with Sadie and her television.

I was just settling on my bed with the *TV Guide* when Nancy's phone rang. A minute later she opened my door and said, "Front and center, Tab. The police are here. They want you at the house."

·5·

"The police" turned out to be policeman, singular. Turner introduced me as his general assistant, Miss Trost, which made me wonder fleetingly when I'd been promoted from kennel girl.

"Tabby, this is Detective Sergeant Holmes, from the

Katonah Police. He just wants to ask you a few questions."

One of my worst faults is that my sense of humor isn't controlled by decency. It was all I could do to keep from asking Holmes where Dr. Watson was tonight. But one look at this Holmes told me that sparkling wit was not going to sit well with him. He was an absolute deadpan, possibly not even aware that Holmes was a humorous name for a detective to have. Or maybe he was just plain sick of Sherlock jokes. At any rate, I managed to keep my face straight as I shook his hand and followed him from the formal living room, where everyone was gathered, across the entrance hall into the equally formal dining room.

This Holmes didn't look much like Sherlock. He was smallish, with a receding chin that he really should have covered with a beard. He'd have been a totally forgettable-looking man except for his hair, which was thick and wavy and a clear, bright silver. I guessed it was his pride. It looked at least as well groomed as our champion show dogs.

He motioned me into a chair at one corner of the dining table, and he sat across the corner from me. Since the chairs were already angled out, I assumed I was not the first one to be questioned in here. Probably the last, kennel girls being kennel girls even when you call them general assistants.

"Now then, miss, uh, Tabby, is it?"

"Tabitha Trost."

"Yes. Well now, you live here, is that right?"

26

"Yes and no. Does that answer your question?"

He gave me a scathing look, and I shrank. He was right. This was no time for frivolity.

"Sorry," I said. "I'm not used to this kind of thing. I stay here during the summer, because Nancy, that's the kennel manager, goes on long show trips during the summer, so I take care of the kennel while she's gone. And then I come out weekends in the spring and fall, when she's away on show trips. But officially I live at home. With my parents."

"Which is?" He was taking notes in a notebook. That made me feel important.

"Which is 1432 Canon, Katonah. Richard Trost is my father. He's assistant manager at Corby's Tire and Transmission Center."

Holmes had stopped writing. I guess my background didn't warrant a notebook page after all. "All right now, miss, er, Trost, tell me what happened this afternoon. Just tell me everything, in your own words."

Again I had to fight a sudden impulse to giggle helplessly. He sounded so much like a television detective that I was sure he got his lines straight from the tube. Making my face serious, I recited from the same script.

"It all started when I met the victim, the intended victim, that is, at the airport this afternoon. Turner asked me to pick them up, since of course he can't drive. So I run errands like that for him all the time. So I picked up the Quinns and brought them here. I helped them upstairs with their luggage—"

27

"Was anyone else with you when you went upstairs to their room?"

Knowing he already knew all this stuff, I went on reciting. "Yes. Turner came up, well, not with us but a minute or two later. He came in right after Louise found the note in the flowers. She read it first, then Ted read it, and then I did."

"Why did you read the note?" he asked sharply, like a TV detective hitting on a key point.

"Because Mr. and Mrs. Quinn were both standing there looking pole-axed. I was curious, so I went over and read the note over Ted's shoulder. Mr. Quinn. And then Turner came in to see if they needed anything, and I read the note out loud, to him."

"Did he seem surprised? Turner?"

"Well, of course he seemed surprised. I mean, come on. Your house guest finds a note threatening murder stuck in his welcome bouquet—of course you're going to be surprised."

He looked at me silently, and I went on more seriously. "Oh. You mean he might not have been surprised because he might have put it there himself?" I shook my head. "He wouldn't do something like that. He can be kind of moody sometimes, but he'd never . . . why would he . . . I mean, he was the one who hired Ted to judge in the first place. And he's not even showing any dogs at this show."

Again Holmes got a sharp-detective look on his face. "You say it was Turner Quinn who arranged for his brother to come here to judge this dog show?"

For the first time I had the shivery feeling of getting into something serious here. "Well, no, not exactly. Turner is president of the regional Springer Club, which is hosting the National Show. A different regional club hosts the National every year. They try to have the National in different parts of the country each year, to give local exhibitors a fair chance, see. This year it was the east coast's turn, and this year Turner happened to be president. But show arrangements are made a good year in advance, and it's the whole show committee that votes on judges."

"But Turner Quinn would certainly have had a powerful voice in selecting judges, right?"

I shrugged.

"And how did it happen that the show was held here, do you know?"

Again I had the feeling that he'd asked these questions of everybody else and didn't really need to be pumping the kennel help. But what the heck.

"They have shows here all the time. The local kennel club has all-breed matches here twice a year, and the regional Springer Club usually has its fall Specialty here, so this was the logical place for the National. We've got the necessary room for the judging rings, for exhibitors' camping, even for the hunting and tracking tests, which most show sites wouldn't have. And the club doesn't have to pay any rent."

"I see. And wouldn't there have been objections from committee members at the club president wanting to hire his own brother as a judge? I assume the judges are well paid for doing this."

"Oh, no, nobody thought anything about that. Everyone in springers knows Turner and Ted can't stand each other."

Oops.

I flushed, and Holmes gave me a cynical look. He obviously already knew the brothers didn't get along, but I still felt like a fool.

"Your boss is an excellent typist, isn't that right?" Holmes fired at me. It would have been stupid to deny it.

"And how many typewriters are there on the place?"

"Just the one. In the kennel. Turner uses that if he wants to type something."

"And what does he type?"

I shrugged. "Lists sometimes. Or letters, club correspondence or maybe an inquiry about a dog, although Nancy usually does the kennel correspondence. I type pedigrees sometimes. That's about all that typewriter is used for."

"Wouldn't it be easier for your boss to dictate his correspondence to you, or to a secretary?"

Again I shrugged. "There's not that much to do. Of course, before he retired he used secretaries for his business. But he likes to type, and it's the easiest way for him to leave notes around the house"—I was getting in deep again—"for Mrs. Jasper to get something special at the market, or for me or Nancy to remember to do something with the dogs. Order a vaccine or whatever."

There was silence while he made notes. I asked, "Was Ted's note written on our typewriter?"

"No," Holmes said, "it wasn't."

He released me and I went back to the living room, where no one paid any attention to my presence, so I stayed a while and eavesdropped.

Louise was saying, "Well, you can't just give in to this sort of thing, Teddy. It's ridiculous. It would make you look an absolute fool when the story got out. Any exhibitor who didn't like you could send you a threatening letter, and scare the pants off you, and die laughing."

Stiffly Ted said, "A threat has been made against my life, and you're all treating it like some sort of joke. I'm not obligated to go through with the judging assignment under these circumstances, you know."

Turner, lounging elegantly against the mantle, said with a quirk of a smile, "It's no fun being in this position, is it, brother?"

Ted grew suddenly rigid and I could see, if Turner couldn't, the absolute fury in Ted Quinn's face. In the sudden, loaded silence of the room, his voice sounded harsh.

"Of course I'll judge. I was only pointing out that I'm not obligated to, under the circumstances. AKC would certainly not argue against a switch in judges if it came to that. But I have no intention of being bullied by anonymous threats."

I had the very strong impression that he wanted nothing more than to fold in the face of the threat and resign the judging assignment. I also had the impression that there was something between the brothers, some shared memory, that prevented Ted from capitulating.

I left before anyone became aware of me, and went back to my room. I was undressed and in bed before a delayed realization struck me.

Holmes had said our typewriter wasn't the one used to write the note.

But then, our typewriter had been at Model Printing and Office Supplies for the past three days, getting its innards cleaned. It was the loaner typewriter that had been in the kennel office all week, and Holmes must have taken a typing sample from that to compare with the note.

And thinking of the kennel office, the typewriters, I suddenly remembered the man I'd seen in the office that afternoon, poking around near the typewriter and looking guilty when I came in. Who was he?

Sleep was very slow in coming.

Thursday, June 27

·1·

By eight o'clock the next morning, my kennel chores were done and I was free to enjoy the day, at least until Turner wanted me for something.

It was a beautiful morning. The air was cool and dry, although the sun would be hot in another two hours. I felt airy and full of excitement, as though the day held nothing but fun.

I stood in the road in front of the house and looked around, deciding on a direction. In the field to my right camping exhibitors walked or ran with their dogs in the dewy grass, playing with them and exercising them. Some were cooking breakfast on camp stoves or charcoal grills. Dogs barked, children yelled. A truck from the dog show company superintending the show was just pulling into the ring area with the tenting and ring equipment.

To my left, through the trees that lined the brook, I could see the gathering of the tracking dogs and handlers. I knew from typing up schedules that the first track was scheduled to start at eight.

Behind me, out of sight beyond the house, the hunting test judges and competitors were gathering about now, I guessed, getting ready to work the first dog, testing for steadiness to shot, for ability to find the planted pigeons in the undergrowth, and to retrieve wing-bound birds on land and in the pond at the far side of the field.

I made my choice, and ambled toward the tracking test. A rustic footbridge spanned the stream. I stood on its arch and watched as the first dog and handler approached the number-one track. A half hour ago a track-layer had walked the track, picking up the marker flags left yesterday by the judges, leaving in their place only the scent of his body and the scent of crushed grass and disturbed earth where he walked. The track was invisible now, except for the starting flag and a second flag thirty yards down the track.

The dog was a small liver-and-white bitch, not a good show animal—I could see that from where I stood—but probably loved by the kid who handled her, a boy of about ten or twelve. The dog wore a tracking harness and the requisite forty-foot-long lead.

The two judges stood a little behind the boy, their track maps on their clipboards. "Any time you're ready," the woman judge called cheerfully to the boy.

He put his dog on a down-stay command beside the starting flag, then bent over the dog, pointed to the ground, and said, "Go find it!"

With a lurch the dog was off, sniffing, circling until she was sure she had the track, then pulling her handler in a straight line across the field. The judges followed at a discreet distance behind boy and dog.

The four of them disappeared over a rise in the ground, and I walked on down to where the others stood watching, the boy's parents and several other trackers, along with three or four Spaniel Club members who were on the tracking committee and were working today as track-layers.

Most of the conversations faded as the watchers stretched to see the progress of the track. Suddenly through the silence came a whoop, cheers, yippees, and the boy's parents jumped around and hugged each other. Over the crest of the hill came the team of judges, grinning, and the boy and his dog running and leaping through the grass. Over his head, the boy waved the brown cotton work glove the track-layer had left at the end of the five hundred yards of zigzagged trail.

A successfully completed track, and a new Tracking Dog degree. I grinned along with everyone else, although I didn't know the family.

The party moved off down the field toward the starting flags for track two, but there was a delay in starting. The track had not yet aged the necessary half hour. I found the man who was tracking chairman, although I couldn't remember his name, and asked him if he needed anything. I was hoping they'd let me lay one of the tracks, but he said no, everything was under control.

"Which is more than you can say for the conformation end of it," he added. "I hear you're murdering off judges up there."

He said it lightly, but the woman standing next to him was incensed. "What was all that about, anyhow? We heard something about a threat to kill one of the judges if he did his judging assignment. There wasn't any truth to that, was there?"

Before I could answer, the man chuckled. "What's so surprising about that, Linda? Can you think of anybody you'd rather kill than a dog-show judge? I seem to recall you making a few threats along those lines, yourself, after the Cherry Blossom Circuit last spring. Remember, when old what's-his-name—you know, the one who always wears white slacks—put up that hairless wonder from the Bred-By class over your Open Bitch. I thought you were going to do him in, right there in front of God and everybody."

"Oh, well, that's different," the woman snipped. "This was the real thing. Wasn't it?" she said to me.

"Probably not," I assured her. "The police did come out and ask a few questions, but I don't think anybody's taking it very seriously. I mean, come on. Nobody actually kills judges, however tempting the thought may be."

The woman asked me, "Quinn is going to judge, then, as scheduled?"

I nodded. "That's the plan."

"Damn. I've got a bitch entered who'd do a lot better

under Tomas. Oh well, we just wanted to bring an entry to the National. We don't really expect to do anything in competition like this. It's just exciting to be here."

I left them as soon as I'd watched the second dog start his track. Crossing the footbridge and the road, I jumped the low stone wall and began to wander down to the circle of vans and motor homes. Partly I was playing hostess of the manor, looking for people who might need something or who might have questions. But mostly I was looking for a face.

Lying in bed last night I'd decided two things: I'd mention the switched typewriters only if Holmes asked me about it directly, so that evasion would be dangerous. And, I would find out the identity of the man who had been messing around in the office yesterday and just possibly typing a note on our typewriter. The house had been empty and unlocked much of the afternoon yesterday. It wouldn't have been hard for someone to type a note on Turner's typewriter, thus incriminating him, and then slip it into the flowers when they were delivered, or even to go upstairs and put the note in the Quinns' room.

I was reasonably sure the man was here for the show, so he shouldn't be hard to find. He'd been dressed neatly, more like a professional dog handler than like someone doing tracking or hunting tests.

Casually, I ambled around the field, getting my sneakers and feet soaked in the grass, pausing in front of exercise pens full of bouncing springers. They aren't called springers for nothing. Several almost knocked over their wire exercise pens in their eagerness to get at my patting hands.

I saw a lot of beautiful dogs and a lot of sleepy, unshaven men sitting or standing around outside their rigs, watching over their dogs or their frying breakfasts. I saw women in shorts and hair rollers and grooming aprons. But I didn't see my man.

When I'd covered the whole motor-home circle I angled toward the center of the field, where the rings were being set up. The show superintendent's crews were erecting a long open-sided tent of blue-and-gold-striped canvas down the center of the ring area. The four rings would spread out, two on each side, from the tent, so that at least one side of each ring would be shaded by the canvas. Off to the side of the ring area a second tent was being stretched out across the grass. That would be the grooming tent, I knew. Electric cables were being installed there, so exhibitors could do last-minute touchups with clippers and blow-dryers.

As I started up the slope toward the kennel, thinking I'd better check in with Turner in case he needed me, I saw my man, at last. He was talking to Nancy and gesturing angrily. When I approached, he left and stomped away toward the motor-home area.

"Who was that?" I asked her.

"Phil Deitz," she snapped. "Pain-in-the-butt Deitz."

"What was he mad about?"

"Oh, who knows? He's just one of those malcontents. Said the premium list promised electrical hookups for motor homes, and now he gets here and finds out he has

38

to rough it, and he can't groom six dogs without electricity. I told him the premium list just said motor home camping available, it did not promise hookups, and why didn't he just set up his tables in the grooming tent, like everybody else. He was less than thrilled at that idea." We turned and walked together, back toward the comfort of our own kennel. "Nan?"

"Present."

"That guy, Deitz? He wouldn't have any reason to threaten Ted Quinn, would he?"

She stopped walking to stare at me, scoffing at first, then suddenly thoughtful. "He might."

·2·

The sun was strong enough by now to push us toward the only shade handy, a large square truck labeled FOLEY DOG SHOWS. It was from this truck that the Foley crews had unloaded the tenting and the ring fencing. For now, the crews were working elsewhere and the truck stood alone.

In its shade we stopped, turned, aimed our faces toward the activity in the ring area, instinctively camouflaging our topic.

Nancy hunched her shoulders and jammed her hands into her slacks pockets. "Old Phil wants Best in Show here pretty badly, and he's got a dog that could do it, if Sally were judging Best in Show instead of Ted. For one thing, it's Sally's kind of dog. Doesn't carry a lot of coat, but he's a moving fool. Goes like an express train. That Grampa Jones dog; you've seen pictures of him."

I remembered the name, at any rate. All the big breeders ran full-page ads in the *Springer Quarterly,* touting their current winners. I remembered that the pictures of Champion Redstone's Grampa Jones had hillbilly sketches in the background behind the dog's photo—an Ozark cabin, as I recalled.

Nancy went on. "This Grampa Jones dog is a good one, but not superstar quality. It'd take a judge like Sally to put him up, and even then, in an entry like we've got here, with something like sixty champions in the Best of Breed class, chances are the dog would be overlooked. With Ted judging, Phil's dog doesn't have a prayer."

I scowled thoughtfully. "That doesn't seem like enough of a reason, though, for Phil to have written that note."

"Well, maybe old Phil's got something set up with Sally. Seems to me they used to have a thing going, years ago before Phil got married. According to scuttlebutt, Phil married money. Daughter of a rich client."

"Phil is a professional handler, then?" I asked.

Nancy nodded. "From the Chicago area. Not one of the most successful handlers in the business. Seems to me his wife's family was his big bread-and-butter client, and they were so furious about their only daughter marrying a dog handler that they disinherited the daughter and gave their dogs to Tom Waterbury, who has done a ton of winning with them and more or less left old Phil at the starting gate."

I knew enough about dog-show handlers, from listening to Nancy and Turner, to know it was an iffy business at best. Nancy served as private handler to Turner, showing his dogs for him, sending in entries, keeping records, all of the necessary details. But Nancy had job security, a paycheck, and a home whether her dogs won or lost.

Handlers like Phil carried a load of expenses on their shoulders. They had to have kennels, motor homes, someone to take care of the at-home dogs while they were on the road, money to feed a big hungry motor home that was on the road every weekend all year. They charged about fifty dollars per show, per dog, about enough to cover travel expenses if they had a string of six or more dogs. But in order to make any real profit, they had to have dogs good enough to win bonus fees, a hundred dollars for a Best of Breed win, another hundred for a Group placing, maybe five hundred for Best in Show.

To get those top-level wins, they had to be successful enough to attract the best dogs. And in order to attract the best dogs, they had to have a winning track record. It was a tough business to rise in, and dirty tricks were not unheard-of. Nancy and Turner had talked casually about handlers rigging wins in various ways—pulling strings with show-host clubs to get a certain judge hired, and letting the judge know about it so that the judge could repay the favor by giving the handler a Group win. That sort of thing. Sending cases of scotch at Christmas to judges who were known to show their gratitude in the ring.

I said, "But Nancy, handlers don't really do things like sending that note, do they?"

She sniffed. "Well, I've never heard of it before. I've known one or two cases where somebody saw a judge coming out of the wrong motel room in the middle of the night, and the next day got a surprise win from that judge as a sort of keep-your-mouth-shut thing. And I've heard old-timers talk about years ago, when the handlers all traveled together in railroad cars. Some of those old boys played pretty rough, stealing each other's dogs, sometimes even poisoning or drugging or laming the other guy's dogs. But I don't think anything like that goes on anymore. For one thing, there used to be big cash prizes in the early days. Now you're lucky if you even get a trophy ashtray. It's all ego, now. Nobody does it for money."

The Foley crews had both of the tents up now and had begun setting up the white lattice-type fencing around the four big rings. Nancy spotted something that needed her attention and left me to lope across the grass toward the rings.

I wandered back toward the house, conscious that the morning was passing and Turner might want me for something.

I was halfway up the sloping lawn when a man's voice called, "Oh, young lady."

I turned with a hostessy smile, expecting to give directions to the camping area or the portable restrooms that had been delivered yesterday—four turquoise fiberglass huts shaped like walk-in refrigerators.

42

But the call came from the silver-coiffed Detective Holmes. He was standing in the parking area, hands in pockets, apparently just a casual observer of the goings-on. I went over to him.

"Let's see, your name was . . ." he said.

"Tabby Trost. General assistant. Actually kennel girl."

"Oh, yes. Tabby. How are things going this morning?" He gestured toward the tents and rings, but I knew better than to think he was asking about the dog show.

"Fine," I said.

"And have you thought of anything more that you might add to what you told me last night? Any detail at all?"

I did some quick metal weighing. Turner was my boss and I owed him my first loyalty. But on the other hand, this was a serious thing, and I wasn't entirely sure I wasn't breaking a law myself by withholding information.

"I did think of something after I went to bed last night," I said finally. "That typewriter in our office? That is our typewriter, but it was at the repair place all week getting cleaned. We had a different one, a loaner, from Monday to yesterday afternoon, if that makes any difference."

I could tell by the way he stiffened, like a hunting dog on point, that I'd told him something important.

"And this loaner came from?"

"Uh, Model Printing in Katonah, on the main street there just north of the bank."

"Would you be able to identify the machine if you saw it?" he snapped.

"Yeah, I could. It was a Smith Corona, kind of green-ish-blue with cream-colored keys, and the question mark key always stuck when you hit it."

Abruptly he turned, gripped my elbow as if he thought I was going to make my getaway, and steered me toward an anonymous-looking white sedan parked near the kennel office. "Let's run into town and take a look at that typewriter."

"Okay, but I have to tell Turner I'm going. He depends on me to be where he can yell for me."

We found Turner in the kennel office, barking orders into the phone. I gathered he was talking to the caterers. Tonight was the judges' banquet, here in Turner's dining room, and it sounded like there was a problem with the shrimp.

When he finally slammed down the phone, I said, "Turner, uh, Detective Holmes is here, and he wants me to run into town with him. It'll only take a few minutes. Is that okay?"

He rose and came around the desk toward us, unsnapping his white cane to its full length although he didn't need it in the familiar office. That meant he was mad, and the cane was some sort of weapon for him, at least in his mind.

He jabbed it in the direction of our breathing, and snapped, "What are you doing, Holmes, arresting my kennel girl now? Do you have any idea how inconvenient all this is? I have a four-hundred-dog show to put on here, a four-day event with exhibitors and judges coming from all over this country and beyond. I am not able to do it unassisted," he said in a rather nasty and pointed reference to his blindness. "I need Tabby here with me."

Holmes pulled himself up an inch taller, not that Turner could see the difference of course. "This is official business, Quinn. I'll have her back as soon as possible."

In my peacemaker voice I said, "He just wants me to identify that loaner typewriter we were using this week. I'll be back in a half hour, tops."

I thought his face darkened for an instant, at the mention of the typewriter, but his expression smoothed so fast I wasn't sure I'd seen anything after all. Waving his cane dangerously close to our faces, Turner motioned us away.

·3·

I have to admit it was a little bit exciting to be aiding in a police investigation, as they say on television, even though my help was hardly necessary. Model Printing was a little place with only a few typewriters sitting around. The owner pointed out our loaner Smith Corona, which was still sitting where I'd dumped it yesterday afternoon, on a shelf in the repair area. I typed a little on it, checked the sticking key, and pronounced it our loaner. Then Holmes typed on it—not words, just hitting every key in turn. He folded away his sample, stuck it in his pocket, and steered me back out to the car.

I hoped he might try to pry information out of me by taking me to Taco John's for lunch. They have the best nachos in the world. But I guess that only happens on television. What I got was a ride home, period.

On the way I remembered the other thing I'd planned to tell Holmes. I decided to tell him, nachos or not.

"I did think of somebody who could have used that typewriter, and who might have wanted to scare Ted," I said. "He's one of the handlers who's here for the show. Phil Deitz is his name. Yesterday I caught him in the office, kind of standing over my desk where the typewriter was. I didn't know who he was then, I just thought he looked kind of guilty when I caught him in there poking around."

"Deitz?" Holmes pulled his little notebook from his shirt pocket and flipped it open on his knee.

"I think it's D-e-i-t-z. He's from around Chicago somewhere, and I heard this morning that he needs to win this show pretty badly and that his dog would have a much better chance under the other judge than under Ted."

Holmes frowned thoughtfully as he tucked away the notebook. Traffic was light on this little blacktop road. He slowed the car to forty-five, probably so we'd have more talking time before we got home, I guessed.

"How would anyone know who the substitute judge would be if the scheduled judge didn't show up?" he asked.

"Well, in a case like this, the logical substitute would be the other judge. See, according to AKC regulations, a judge is only allowed to do a certain number of dogs in a day. I think the limit is two hundred, but I'm not sure about that. So, for this show, which is the National Specialty . . ."

"Specialty?" he interrupted.

"That's a show for only one breed. Springer spaniels in this case. As opposed to an all-breed show, which would be for—"

"All breeds," he said in unison with me.

"Right. There are specialty breed clubs all around the country—the Chicago Area Springer Spaniel Club, and so on. They each have annual specialty shows, and then every June one of them hosts the National Specialty, which is 'The Biggie.' Whatever dog wins the National is king of the breed for that year."

"I understand," Holmes said. "Go on about the judges."

"Oh. Yeah. So the National usually draws an entry of around three hundred dogs in the conformation division, which is what we're talking about here. They also have obedience trials and tracking and hunting tests, but those are judged by other kinds of judges. Conformation is where the dogs are judged on their physical qualities; how well they conform to the official breed standard.

"So the club hires two conformation judges, and they'll assign the dog classes to one judge, and the bitch classes to the other one. Dog means male, bitch means female."

47

He gave a snort, which I didn't bother to interpret.

"Then, besides the male and female classes, there's a huge Best of Breed class where they take the top non-champion male and female and add them in with this whole herd of champions, of both sexes, and everybody goes for the big win—Best in Show. They usually assign Best in Show to whichever of the two judges has more prestige."

"In this case, Ted Quinn?"

I nodded. "I think mainly his prestige comes from the fact that he lives in England. That always seems more impressive than bringing a judge from New Jersey. Lots of people don't realize Ted is really an American, so they get all impressed with the idea of showing under a British judge."

"But if Ted were to withdraw, what would happen then?"

"Well, if he withdrew from the whole judging assignment, they'd have to bring in a new judge because Sally Tomas couldn't judge all the classes by herself. But that note just said 'Don't judge Best in Show,' so if Ted went ahead and judged his other classes and just backed out of the Best in Show class, then the logical thing would be for Sally to do that one class."

"And you think this—what was his name, Deitz?—would be sure enough of winning it with Sally judging, and would want to win it badly enough, to take desperate measures?"

"I don't know. How should I know? I'm just a kid. I just work in the kennel. All I'm saying is what Nancy told me about Phil Deitz. I just thought you should know about him, that's all."

I was starving by the time I got back to the kennel. The office was empty, which was a relief. Turner did have a way of sending me on little errands just when I was trying to get upstairs to a meal. He never seemed to get hungry himself, and I guess he forgot that other people did.

I checked the dogs, gave the newly weaned puppies their noon gruel, then bolted upstairs to the apartment. Nancy wasn't there, so I made a couple of fat bologna-and-cheese sandwiches with tomato and lettuce and munched them down.

Back outdoors again, I looked for Turner and found him on the brick terrace at the front of the house. He sat alone, at the glass-and-wrought-iron umbrella table, apparently following the activity around him with his ears.

"Tabby?" he said, as I approached. It always knocked me out, how he could recognize my walk, in sneakers, across soft grass.

"I'm here." I sat in the other chair in the umbrella's shade.

"How did it go in town?" he asked politely.

"Fine. I showed him which typewriter it was, and he took a sample of type from it. I suppose they'll match that sample with the note and see if it was typed on that typewriter. But it wouldn't be. Would it?"

He smiled. I really liked old Turner when he smiled, maybe because he didn't do it all that often. "Not unless you or I or Nancy wrote it. I didn't, you didn't, and I doubt that Nancy did."

"Somebody else could have," I said. "That office is unlocked, we're in and out of it all day, and there are plenty of other people wandering around here. I even caught one of the handlers in there yesterday, Phil Deitz. He was poking around the desk, and he jumped when I came in. He could have been typing on it, and finished before I got there."

Turner thought a while, then said, "What did the paper look like, Tab? The note."

I frowned and tried to remember. "It looked kind of funny. It was white paper, kind of thick and bumpy, like our kennel stationery. Bond? Is that what it's called? It looked kind of like that."

"What was funny about it, then?" he asked.

I wasn't sure. I called up the memory of the paper as I'd seen it in Ted's hands, a square of white, folded twice to fit into the florist's envelope.

"It was square," I said finally. "But biggish square, Not rectangular like stationery or note paper or anything like that. It was about the size that business stationery is wide, but it was square."

We sat silently while I thought about that. Suddenly I said, "It looked like it could have been business stationery with the top cut off. You know, the letterhead or whatever you call it, across the top of business stationery, with names and addresses and a design?"

Our own kennel stationery said "Quintessence, English Springer Spaniels," across the top, with our address and phone number and a small embossed profile of a springer in the center. Take a piece of that, cut off the identifying top couple of inches, and you'd have a square of plain, white bond paper, just like that note.

I opened my mouth to tell Turner, but hesitated, looking at him. His face was handsome in profile, his sightless eyes staring toward the distant sounds of the Foley crew and the camping families. There was something going on inside that head with its funny halfway-back hairline and its clearcut features. I could almost see the mental activity.

"Don't stare at me, Tabby," he said, with a note of teasing warmth in his voice.

"How can you tell?" I demanded. His abilities always amazed me.

"I can feel it. I can feel you sitting there wondering if I wrote that note."

"Well? Did you?"

He smiled sadly, and shook his head. "I thought you knew me better than that, by now."

"I don't know you at all," I shot back. "I have no idea why you hate Ted, for one thing."

His smile hardened. "That's not something I talk about with the kennel help."

I got up in a huff and started across the terrace.

"Tab." His voice stopped me like a leash around my neck. "I want you at the banquet tonight. Have you got something decent to wear? Come down about six; you can help the caterers get set up."

"Yes sir." I saluted, not entirely sure he didn't know I'd made the semidefiant gesture.

·4·

Promptly at six I reported for duty in the dining room. I'd borrowed the Cimarron during the mid-afternoon lull and driven home for my best dress and panty hose and heels. Until now, my kennel-girl duties hadn't required anything more than jeans.

It had been a quiet afternoon. Ted and Louise had spent it watching the hunting tests in the back fields, and Turner had stayed enthroned on the terrace, keeping an ear on things, so to speak. Nancy had groomed dogs all afternoon; it was her way of escaping from people. I'd run home for my dress-up clothes, then wandered aimlessly most of the afternoon, from tracking test to hunting test to the rings and camping areas, having nothing special to do, but preferring to stay away from Turner as much as possible.

Walking into the dining room, I felt as silly as I always did in hose and heels, like a little girl playing dress up. The panty hose never quite stayed up as high as they were supposed to, and the blue linen dress wrinkled across the front, under my stomach bulge, and probably wrinkled across the seat, too, but I couldn't see back there so I didn't worry about it. And I could never walk normally in heels. My feet came down stiff and clumpy no matter how much I tried to arch my instep.

52

All in all, I envied Nancy, who had been invited to the dinner but who'd had the guts to tell Turner she'd be busy with the kennel work. I'd rather have been with the woofers myself just then, dressed in civilized clothes. Jeans and sneakers and a ratty T-shirt.

But Turner needed a gofer and I was elected. He was already there, looking spiffy in tan slacks and a brown tweed sport jacket with a dark-brown silk turtleneck under it. I knew Turner well enough to know he took a vengeful sort of pride in his appearance, as though he were defying the world to make allowances for his blindness. He shaved more carefully than most sighted men, and spent more time selecting his outfits, recognizing each jacket or sweater or shirt by its feel. I didn't always like the guy, but I admired him ceaselessly.

"I'm here," I said. He was standing behind a chair midway down the long dining table, his hands resting on the knobs of the chair back.

It was a large dining room for a private home, large and square, with a fireplace and floor-to-ceiling windows looking out over the stream and the tracking test fields. The table was augmented tonight by two additional folding tables from the caterer, so that the tables made an unbroken L along two sides of the room. Expensive, white linen cloths covered the tables, and masses of low floral arrangements were set every few yards along the tables.

"Tab," Turner said, "read me the place tags, starting at that end, near the door."

I walked along the table and read off the names, which

I'd typed earlier in the week onto thick creamy cards. Each card leaned against a small pewter springer figure, souvenir table favors. Ordered by me, weeks ago.

"Jim Tomas, Sally Tomas. Louise Quinn, Ted Quinn, you. Me, Irene Abernathy, Edward Abernathy." I continued down the length of the tables, naming the obedience, tracking, and hunting test judges and their spouses and half a dozen show-committee members from the Springer Club.

"Fine," Turner said. "Do the flowers look all right?"

"Beautiful. Blue daisies, pink carnations, pink and white baby's breath, some little yellow things, I don't know what they are. Want me to check for notes?"

Oops. That was too flippant. He gave me a look that would curdle milk and sent me to the kitchen to see if the caterers were having any problems. They weren't.

When I got back the room was filling up. I hung around close to Turner's right elbow where he could get me if he needed me. Ted and Louise were there, Ted looking sunburned and hearty, fake-hearty in my opinion, Louise looking slightly bleary. Too much jet lag? Or did she have a bottle stashed away upstairs, I wondered. Her lips were painted on slightly unevenly, one bump higher than the other one. When our eyes met I smiled, and she smiled back in a fuzzy way, as though she didn't quite remember where we'd met.

Sally Tomas made her entrance, followed by husband Jim who was half a head shorter than she and looked as though his growth was stunted from standing in his wife's

54

shadow. She was a big Nordic-looking blond. Statuesque was the word that came to mind. Her voice was deep and strong, dominating the room. As she moved toward Ted and Louise I had the impression that she felt the same way I did about panty hose and shoes higher than ground level. Her natural stride was obviously being hobbled.

The other couples came in a clot, the hunting and tracking judges looking windblown and outdoorsy even in dress-up clothes. The club members sifted in and circulated, eager to make personal contact with judges who might remember them kindly someday in the show ring. Among them was Irene Abernathy, the titular show chairperson.

I say titular, although I'm not entirely sure what it means, because actually Turner was putting on this show, no matter who was named show chairman. But Mrs. A. did look like a show chairperson. She was a stoutly packed woman in some sort of drifty, flowery dress with a big flowered hat on her hair, which was interesting in itself. The hair, that is. It was a sort of sunset-pink color, not designed by Ma Nature, I'd bet the farm on that. Oh well, she was a nice lady. Most of the time she had no idea what was going on, but she was a nice lady.

She talked to me as if I were a real person, which no one else in the room had done. In fact she talked to me through most of the dinner. She was on my right, Turner was on my left, and Ted was beyond him. Turner didn't talk at all through dinner, except when Mrs. Abernathy leaned behind me to ask him something or tell him something.

When we'd finished eating the caterer came and whispered something to Turner. I heard him murmur, "No, wait a few minutes, until we start the videotape."

He stood up then and made a charming short speech of welcome, thanking committee members, complimenting the tracking and hunting test judges, who had done their stint today and would be leaving tomorrow.

Then Sally stood and told a few funny stories about previous Nationals. Finally, Ted stood and cleared his throat.

"I'm not going to make a speech here. I understand we have a videotape of last year's National, compliments of the American Springer Spaniel Association, and I'm sure we'd all rather watch that than listen to me give a long-winded speech."

Polite laughter.

"I just want to say, some of you may have heard rumors about a little unpleasantness we had here yesterday, regarding my judging of Best in Show on Sunday. It was a childish prank, which I'm sure none of us is taking seriously. I'm going on record here and now, assuring you all that I will complete my judging assignment as planned."

He sat down to applause and murmurs.

"Tabby," Turner said, and nodded toward the large-screen television set we'd rented for the evening. It was on the wall across from our stretch of table.

I got up and went to the VCR under the television,

and inserted the tape Mrs. Abernathy had brought with her. Highlights of last year's National Specialty. As the picture came on, I turned off the room lights and sat on the floor where I had a clear view of the set.

While the tape ran, I heard the soft sounds of the caterer's crew clearing dinner dishes and setting out dessert plates. I wanted to get back to my chair and my dessert, but hesitated to stand up and block people's view of the screen, so I stayed where I was.

A few minutes later there was an angry gasp behind me, and Ted's voice sputtered, "What in hell is this?"

"Tabby," Turner called.

I crawled to the VCR, punched the STOP button, and turned on the wall light switch.

Ted Quinn was staring stupidly at a small square of paper that was propped against his block of chocolate rum cake. I crowded in with everyone else, and stared as stupidly as he had.

It was another typed note, very brief this time. "Do not judge B.I.S." And Scotch-taped onto the note, below the typed line, was . . . I looked again.

A bullet.

·5·

Turner sent me scurrying into the kitchen to call Detective Holmes and to warn the caterers not to leave until the police got there. I made the call and explained the situation to the caterer, who promptly burst into tears.

She was a youngish woman, a recent divorcée trying to make a living with her catering business and employing only her two teenage daughters as helpers. I knew the girls slightly, from school, and I had recommended her for this dinner. Her name was Mrs. Beattie. She struck me as a very nervous, timid type, and I was sure neither she nor either of her daughters knew anything about the note and bullet. Still, they huddled together in the middle of the kitchen looking terrified. What a pair of wimps, I thought, eyeing the daughters.

In the dining room tension lay heavy over the conversations. Everyone looked up at me as I swung through the kitchen door and resumed my seat beside Turner.

"The police are on their way," I said. "Nobody's supposed to leave till they get here."

That sounded overly dramatic, even to me. After all, there was no murdered corpse lying on the rug, nothing but a note, which might or might not be serious.

Still, I thought, looking sideways at the note with its attached bullet lying on the table beside Turner's cake plate, this one did look serious. That bullet . . . I shivered, and imagined what Ted must be feeling when he looked at it. Imagining it piercing his heart . . .

Ted did not look at all well. Hoist on his own petard, I realized suddenly. He'd just made his brave public declaration that he wasn't afraid of threats and would judge Best in Show no matter what. Now, the first note, which might well have been a prank, was underscored by this one, which did not look like a prank at all.

Abruptly, Glen Field, the hunting test judge, rose and

came around the table to peer down at the note. He reached to touch it, remembered that he shouldn't, but pointed to the bullet.

"That's a pistol blank," he said. "That's what we've been firing all day for the steady-to-shot tests."

He got a funny look on his face and went back to his seat with an expression as guilty as if he'd been accused.

As an automatic reflex I picked up my fork and picked at my cube of chocolate rum cake, but I had neither the desire nor the guts to eat any of it. No one else was eating.

I looked around the room slowly, casually, with the feeling that everyone else was doing the same thing. Someone in this room had planted that note, while the lights were turned off for the videotape.

Who?

If Mrs. Beattie or her daughters didn't serve the note with the cake, from the kitchen, then someone had to have slipped it onto Ted's plate within a few minutes after the cake plates were served.

Turner was sitting next to Ted, and so was Louise. Either of them could have done it easily, if the note had been prepared ahead of time. And it would have to have been, I realized. It was typed, and the bullet had required Scotch tape. The thing was put together ahead of time and carried in in a pocket . . . or a purse.

Who else was close enough? Sally Tomas was beyond Louise, and I was beyond Turner, except that I hadn't been sitting at the table when the note was planted; I'd been sitting on the floor near the television.

Detective Holmes came in a few minutes later, not ringing the doorbell, just walking straight into the dining room carrying authority with him like a shield. He told us to do what we were already doing, sitting in our dinner chairs and nobody leaving the room.

He studied the note minutely, then slipped it into a plastic Baggie and tucked it away in his pocket. He paced around the room, studying the arrangement of tables and doors. He went into the kitchen and talked for several minutes with the Beatties.

When he came back he asked us all to resume our exact positions at the time the desserts were served. I sat back down on the floor—not an easy maneuver in a straight skirt and half-mast panty hose, let me add.

Holmes said, "All right, young lady, turn on whatever it was you were watching."

Until now the television screen had been black-and-white dancing dots and a static background hum. Nobody had noticed. I punched the VCR's PLAY button, and a ring full of springer spaniel puppies replaced the dancing dots. Last year's Puppy Sweepstakes finals. Holmes snapped off the room lights.

I turned around and looked at the table where Ted and family sat. That part of the room was very dark. Up front, where I sat, the moving blue-white light from the TV screen outlined forms and faces, but back along the wall where Turner and the Quinns sat, it was almost totally dark.

For the first time I noticed something that should have struck me when I first came into the dining room, except that I was distracted by my efforts to walk normally in these damned shoes. The heavy damask drapes were closed over the windows with the stream view. If part of my mind had noticed it, I'd probably assumed that was the way formal dinners were done in ritzy houses like this.

Now, I wondered. It was nine now. It had been eight-thirty or thereabouts when dessert was served, and that's still twilight on a June evening. If the drapes had been open, there behind our table, it would have been much harder for an unseen hand to slip a note onto a cake plate, even with everyone watching the videotape.

Great minds often run in the same channel. Detective Holmes said, "Whose idea was it to close those drapes?"

Turner smiled. "Guilty. Actually we always closed the drapes at dinner, didn't we, Ted? At least in summer. The setting sun makes an unpleasant glare in people's faces otherwise."

Holmes looked keenly at Ted, who nodded reluctantly. I was studying Ted's face at that moment, and I saw what perhaps no one else in the room saw except Holmes. Ted shot his brother a look so venomous that I knew, in that instant, Ted believed the note came from Turner.

Holmes didn't take us into a separate room for questioning this time, he simply took down the names of everyone in the room and asked us the one big question. Did anyone know of anyone in this room who was near Ted during those few moments after the cake was served?

The room was silent. In the mounting tension Louise said suddenly, "It wasn't me. I didn't put it there."

No one said you did, idiot, I thought.

Turner said nothing.

Jim Tomas cleared his throat and said, "Well, actually, uh, Sally . . ."

We all turned and looked at Sally. She flushed a dark red, and I had the impression her husband was going to catch it, later. "Well, yes," she said. "I did go out to the rest room just before the videotape started, and I guess I came back around there, behind their chairs." She motioned toward Ted. "I didn't want to block anybody's view of the screen."

"I see," Holmes said quietly. "And were you at the hunting tests at any time today, or in that area?"

"Well, yes, a while this morning." Her voice was huffy, and she had the voice to do it with, too. "Jim and I walked around there a little bit. So did most of the people here." She waved toward the obedience judges and the club members.

It was true. Any number of people could have picked up an expended shell from the judges' pistols. Sally, or Louise, or almost anyone.

And most of them could have watched for a chance and slipped into the kennel office and used the typewriter and Scotch tape. The door was unlocked, since I'd been out running around most of the day and so had Nancy. And Turner had spent the day on the terrace.

When he'd finished with the questioning, Holmes said to Ted, "If I were you, Mr. Quinn, I believe I'd give up on the idea of judging this show. No sense taking risks."

Louise stood up then, pulling Ted up with her. "My husband is not a coward, Detective Holmes. He said he would judge, and he will judge. If dog-show judges gave in to every irate exhibitor who felt like threatening them, we'd never have any dog shows."

I sucked in my breath and squelched a grin. Her statement certainly didn't say much for the popularity of her husband's judging.

Turner stood also, and said, "Of course Ted will complete his judging assignment. The club has gone to great expense to fly him and his wife over from England. And judging Best in Show at the National Specialty is an honor many judges would kill for. Speaking figuratively, of course. Ted has announced that he will judge, and he will judge."

Ted looked sick.

We were all excused after that, and most of the guests scattered to spread the latest gossip.

I went quietly to my room, ripping off the chafing panty hose and rolling thoughtfully onto my bed.

An honor most judges would kill for?

Would Sally Tomas? Not kill, of course, but threaten? Nah.

Well, probably nah, but then what did I know about Sally Tomas?

Friday, June 28

·1·

It took me so long to fall asleep that I slept a half hour later than usual on Friday morning. Nancy had already eaten and gone down when I went across the landing to the apartment. I inhaled a bowl of cereal and a banana, and clomped down the stairs to my waiting dogs.

Feed puppies, change their newspapers, shake them off my ankles. Feed Supercharge, our current main show dog, who was down in weight. He went off feed every time one of the bitches came into season, and he was entered in three shows next weekend.

Turn all the dogs out into the exercise yards in compatible groups of three or four. Pick up the chunks in the runs and hose down the runs. Check automatic waterer bowls. Sweep up kennel stalls and alleyway and change the blankets in two of the beds, where elderly dogs made mistakes in the night.

While I worked through my morning routine, Nancy did her maintenance grooming, combing out four or five of the kennel dogs and checking them for anything special they might need, ear cleaning or hot-spot salve or whatever. We worked without talking, as we usually did, after I'd filled her in on the unusual table favor at last night's dinner.

She was at the office desk, typing up show entries for August shows, and I was sitting in one of the low chairs by the fireplace trying to decide what to do next, when Detective Holmes came in.

"I'd like to borrow the use of that typewriter for an hour or so," he said. Nancy finished the entry blank she was on and started to get up.

"No, stay there a minute," Holmes said. "Do you have a few sheets of business stationery in the desk there? Fine, yes, that's what I had in mind. Would you take a sheet of that, please, and just type 'The quick brown fox jumped over the lazy dog.'?"

Nancy gave him a look, but typed the sentence. She handed him the paper and left without another word. She went outdoors with a slightly louder than necessary slam of the screen door.

Detective Holmes turned to me and said, "Now you, if you don't mind."

"Me what?"

"Type that same sentence. Take another sheet of that stationery there."

Aha, I thought. "You're testing us all for typing style, aren't you? Or whatever you call it. Can you really tell one person's typing from another's?"

He hesitated, then apparently decided I was harmless. "It can be an aid. It's not as accurate with these electric typewriters as it used to be with manuals, though. Different people have different levels of strength in their various fingers and hit certain letters more strongly than another person would."

I typed "The quick brown fox" and handed him my paper. While he was in a talkative mood, I risked a question.

"Do you have any idea yet who slipped Ted that note last night? Did it have fingerprints on it or anything?"

"These things take time," he said somewhat stiffly.

"Ah." I nodded. "Did you find out anything about Phil Deitz? You said you were going to check into his background."

I thought his expression closed up a fraction at that one.

"It's under investigation," he said. "Now, if you'd like to be of some help, you might just trot out and find me these people and have them come here to the office." He handed me a list.

"You're going to test all these for typing, huh?" I read the list: Turner, Louise, Sally, Phil Deitz, Nancy, me.

"Louise?" I said.

"Wives and husbands are always prime suspects," Holmes said dryly. Another argument in favor of staying single, I thought as I went out into the morning sunlight.

The house people weren't hard to find. I had to ask around at a few motor homes, though, before I located Phil Deitz. His was one of the smaller, older rigs, and the exercise pens beside it looked as though they'd been on the road many years.

I banged on the door, and Deitz appeared, looking haggard and unshaven. He had a stale-sweat odor about him, as though he'd fallen asleep in yesterday's clothes, and maybe he had.

I told him Detective Holmes wanted to see him right away, in the kennel office.

"What the hell for?"

"I believe he's taking samples of different people's typing," I said primly.

"What the hell's he want mine for?"

I said nothing. One good thing about being a kid is that no one really expects you to know anything. Playing dumb is simple.

"Okay, give me a few minutes," he snarled, and slammed the door in my face.

I saw no reason to hang around. He knew the way to the office. I stretched and yawned, and ambled toward the rings.

All four of the rings were busy this morning, with the obedience trial. Two rings held novice classes, which would take all day to judge, I knew. I paused to watch a Novice A dog go through the routine: heel, figure-eight, stand for examination, heel off lead, and come on recall. The dog did well enough until the recall, when a noise outside the ring distracted him at the crucial second, and his handler had to call him a second time, giving him a zero score. Aww, the ringside watchers said.

I found a shady empty chair beside the ring in which the Open B class was being judged. The dog who was working just then sailed over the high jump to retrieve her wooden dumbbell, but got off her stride on the return and, instead of coming back to her handler over the thirty-inch-high barrier, she veered around it and returned to her handler looking guilty. Another zero score.

The man sitting beside me said, "You're sitting in my wife's chair, but that's okay. She won't be back for a while."

The ringside chairs were mostly privately owned lawn chairs. The club had some, but most exhibitors brought their own, or sat on the grass while they waited their turns in the ring.

"Did you come a long way?" I asked, to make conversation.

"Chicago. Well, near Chicago. We always go to the National if we possibly can. My wife and I both teach, so we have summers off, and this is our family vacation. The wife loves this obedience stuff. I don't have the patience for it, myself. Oh, we brought a couple of puppies for Puppy Sweeps, tomorrow, and my son shows in Junior Showmanship. We don't try to get into the big leagues, the open classes or Best in Show. That gets to be too much of a handler's game."

He talked on, telling me more than I wanted to know about each of his dogs. I'd noticed this about people at dog shows. They never ask who I am, or what dogs I

68

might have. I get the feeling they're so hungry to talk about their own dogs they don't want to give the other guy any openings to turn the conversation to his dogs.

When he paused for breath I asked, "If you're from Chicago, you probably know Phil Deitz?"

The man snorted. "Dogless Deitz? Sure, everybody knows him."

"Why dogless?"

"Oh, just a nickname. He's one of those handlers who's always scratching for dogs to handle. He came up to me once and offered to show my champion male, for nothing. Thought he could get a group placement on him under some judge who owed him a favor, I forget who. Said he'd charge me two hundred if he got into the ribbons in the group, and no charge if he didn't."

"You mean it wouldn't matter what dog he was showing? He had an arrangement with the judge ahead of time so he'd win with any dog he took into the group ring?"

"Something like that. At least that was what he told me. I didn't go along with him. A man with his background, I'd just as soon steer clear of, group win or no group win."

"What background, what do you mean?" I sat up.

"Oh, well, he had some kind of Mafia connections in his younger days, at least that's what people say. Before he got into showing dogs. Then he blew himself out of the water as a handler, marrying the daughter of his one and only good client and losing the guy's business. I mean, he had Best in Show winners from that kennel.

Hasn't had anything anywhere near that good since then."

"What about this dog he's showing now?" I said casually. "Has he got a shot at Best in Show here, do you think?"

The man snorted. "Not under Quinn. That man can't see anything but pretty coat. Under a movement judge, he might have a shot."

"Like Sally Tomas?" I asked.

"Like Sally Tomas, but she's not doing Best in Show, is she?"

I shook my head. "Not as of now. But maybe you heard, somebody threatened to shoot Mr. Quinn if he judges, so he might back out."

"Threatened to shoot him?" The man stared at me, then threw back his head and hooted. "My lifelong ambition, to shoot one of those bastards."

When I left him he was still cackling and swatting his knee.

·2·

A full moon brightened the lawns of Quintessence. I sat on the rim of the brick terrace, legs hanging over the edge, back to the crowd.

It wasn't a planned party, I was pretty sure, just people congregating naturally on the terrace on a summer evening. Turner was sitting just behind me, at his umbrella table with Joe Hollis, who would be judging the Puppy Sweepstakes tomorrow. Sitting or standing around the terrace were Ted and Louise, Sally and Jim Tomas, Mrs. Abernathy with her sunset-pink hair practically glowing in the dark, and several other people I didn't know. They seemed to be exhibitors who knew Turner or Ted or Sally, and who were obviously enjoying the chance to rub elbows with the judges. They had materialized from the direction of the motor homes.

Nancy was among them, standing patiently while a woman talked loudly and endlessly about rage syndrome, which apparently infected every breeder's bloodline except hers. She gestured with her cigarette continually under Nancy's nose. Nancy rather pointedly batted away the woman's smoke, but the talker didn't notice.

Mrs. Jasper periodically carried trays of crackers with little things on them out through the French doors, and various bottles were passed around. There was no bar, as such, since Turner didn't drink and hadn't planned to entertain tonight. But apparently the bottles of scotch and vodka were standard equipment in several of the motor homes.

I couldn't help overhearing several conversations, since I was blatantly listening. The subject of Ted's threatening notes was woven regularly through the dog talk. Some people thought it was a crime that a respected judge, a guest in our country as well as in his own home, should be subjected to such treatment. Some thought it was a crime to be paying the taxes we were and still not have a police force that could clean up a little thing like this.

Others seemed unable to refrain from making jokes. "Hey, Ted, who have you been dumping lately? Maybe it's that woman, remember that woman at Atlanta two years ago? That mouthy broad you gave Reserve to, and she threw the ribbon in your face. Remember her? God, I thought I'd die laughing."

Ted smiled, but it was a stiff one. "That was a terrible dog," he said. "I wouldn't have given her Reserve if there'd been anything else in the ring that wasn't total junk. That was one of those best-of-the-worst decisions."

He was trying to act normally, I guessed. I didn't know him well enough to know what normal was, but I figured dignified bonhomie was the image he probably loved to project when socializing with dog folk. I hadn't met a lot of judges, but already I knew there were the ones who went into the profession because they truly loved purebred dogs and had the necessary eye for differentiating fine points. And then there were the ones who were irresistibly drawn to the ego puffery of being a judge. Within his ring, a dog-show judge was omnipotent. He could break hearts, make dreams come true, pay off favors, do almost anything he wanted, with the pointing of one finger. He was accountable to no one for his decisions, and any exhibitor who argued with him could lose the privilege of competing in future dog shows. Hopeful exhibitors flirted with a judge, fought for the honor of meeting his plane or running errands for him. Anyone with a hungry ego could feast for a lifetime on judgehood.

My guess was that Ted Quinn was one of those.

I turned around to watch the crowd, looking for Phil Deitz on the off chance that he might have joined the party. He hadn't. But in turning, my shoulder bumped Turner's chair. His hand came around and found the top of my head.

"Tab. You're still here. Have a dance with me."

I felt a little silly getting up there in my shorts and sandals, but I did, and found Turner a surprisingly good dancer. I hadn't done much close dancing, but within a few steps we'd found our balance, me steering gently away from the edge of the terrace, him doing the actual leading. The music came from the elaborate tape deck in the living room. Mostly Turner listened to Bach on it, but tonight the tapes were big-band stuff that sounded like forties music. I found I liked it.

"So," Turner said over my head. "What do you think of the goings-on, little Tabby-cat?"

He knew I hated that nickname, so he used it when he wanted to needle me. "How should I know what to think? I'm just a lowly kennel girl of the teenager variety. We don't grow brains till we hit twenty-one, remember?"

He gave me a light smack on my bottom. "Don't give me that. Tell me what you think. Who do you suppose has been writing the notes?"

"Not I," I said curtly.

"Nor I?" he asked lightly.

"Nor you. Nor Nancy. I wouldn't swear to anybody else."

I thought I felt him relax slightly. "You're a good girl,

Miss Tabby-cat, even if I do yell at you from time to time."

"That's okay. You yell at everybody."

He chuckled, and traded me for Nancy when the music paused.

I went back to my seat and thought about what he'd said and what I'd said. I told him not I or he or Nancy, but did I say that because I believed it, or because I knew it was what he wanted me to say? I honestly didn't know.

Louise Quinn was dancing very, very closely with Jim Tomas. Embarrassingly close, in my opinion. I looked around to see if their spouses were noticing. Ted was looking the other way, in deep conversation with someone I didn't know. Sally Tomas seemed to have disappeared. Another trip to the rest room, probably.

I couldn't tell whether Jim was enjoying the fact that Louise seemed to be trying to crawl right through him, or whether he was embarrassed and trying to make the best of the situation. He looked red-faced and sweaty, but that could prove either side of the question.

Even to my innocent sixteen-year-old eyes, it looked to me like old Louise was carrying a load. Her laugh was loud, her hair seemed to have a life of its own and was rebelling, and her lips had pretty much disappeared. The fake lip-bumps, that is, not the real lips.

Disgusting woman, I thought. Maybe she's been writing scare notes to old Ted. Maybe she can't stand the old windbag and is trying to make him look silly in front of a lot of important springer people.

The idea was born of my sleepy silliness, but once it had wandered through my head, it left a trail I couldn't help following.

Could Louise have done it? If she'd typed up the two notes ahead of time, at home, say, and had them in her purse . . . and then when they got here and went into their room and she saw the envelope from the florist, she did a sleight-of-hand and exchanged the original welcome note for the poison-pen one in her purse. Of course, she couldn't have known the flowers would be there, but she could have planned to leave the note anywhere in the room.

I tried to remember if there had been time for her to do that when no one was looking, but I honestly couldn't recall.

Certainly she could have picked up the pistol shell casually while they watched the hunting tests yesterday, and certainly she could have found time during the afternoon to tape the shell onto the second note. And it would have been easy enough for her to slip it onto Ted's cake plate.

All possible, I supposed, but not terribly logical. There must be easier ways to humiliate a husband.

Sally still hadn't reappeared an hour later when I decided enough was enough. I slid down off the terrace, told Turner I was leaving, and started around the house toward the kennel and the stairs to my room.

But now that I was up and moving, I found I wasn't quite sleepy enough to want to end the evening. The moonlight was bright enough to make walking easy, at least out in the open. I started down the slope toward the rings. All was quiet and peaceful there. The obedience jumps had been packed away, and the rings were ready for the main events, the conformation judging, which would begin in the morning with Puppy Sweepstakes.

A movement under the trees behind me snagged my vision. A woman was walking very fast, head down, toward the house. She looked up, saw me, hesitated for an instant, then went on. She was tall and blond and was wearing a pale dress. Just like Sally Tomas had been wearing when she disappeared from the group on the terrace.

And she had come out of Phil Deitz's motor home.

Saturday, June 29

·1·

I lay in bed that night trying to gear down my racing mind. I was tired, I wanted to sleep, but they kept chasing one another through my head, like cartoon sheep being counted—all the people who might be threatening Ted Quinn.

There was Turner, but it couldn't be him. He was often moody and sometimes rude and thoughtless, and he had no love for his brother, but still. He was my boss, a man I knew and liked, an intelligent, sophisticated, middle-aged adult. The notes had been so . . . childish. So silly, really. I couldn't see a man like Turner Quinn doing anything that sophomoric.

There was Phil Deitz, Sally Tomas—either or both of the above: Phil, who desperately needed the Best in Show win,

77

and Sally, who was probably willing to give it to him if she did the judging. Sally visiting Phil in his motor home in the dead of night and coming out looking rumpled and guilty. Or was the rumpled and guilty part just my imaginative supposition? But Sally had seen me standing there by the rings; she'd looked right at me in the moonlight and made a small, startled movement, then looked relieved that it was only a kennel girl, nobody important. Nobody likely to tell her husband where she'd been.

There was Sally herself, who might have some unknown reason for wanting to judge Best in Show. But it would have to be an awfully strong reason, I thought. She was a respected judge with a good reputation. She wouldn't risk that by doing something as stupid as writing threatening notes to another judge. No, that didn't make sense.

Maybe there was something in Phil's background that I didn't know about, some kind of pressure he was under, from old Mafia connections. Maybe the owner of the dog Phil was handling was some sort of mobster who thought he could muscle his way into a Best in Show. That would have seemed illogical to me a year ago, but by now I'd been around dog show people enough to know that, for lots of exhibitors, the ego-lust for prestige wins could indeed grow to sickie level.

As I began, finally, to sink toward the edge of sleep, I remembered what Detective Holmes had said about wives and husbands. There was Louise, obviously a drinker, obviously interested in men, very probably disgusted with her silly, cowardly husband. Could she be doing this to needle him or humiliate him or, in some way I didn't understand, to get free from him? She would have no vested interest in whether or not he judged the Best in Show class, but the National Specialty was the focus of the whole springer spaniel world this week, and if Ted chickened out of his judging assignment because he'd gotten a couple of silly notes, he'd be laughed out of the fancy. A hate-filled wife just might . . .

Nah. That didn't make any more sense than any of the other possibilities. None of it made any sense. What it did make was nervous tension. This was the third night in a row I'd had trouble falling asleep, and I was getting tired of it. After all, I reasoned, it wasn't as if I was in any danger myself. Probably nobody was, not even Ted. Certainly not I, so what was I so tense about?

Much later, as I began the final slide down into sleep, a tiny sound jerked me awake.

I lifted my head and stared toward my door. It was opening, opening slowly, an inch at a time. My eyes widened.

The door was opening, but no one was there. No one I could see—

A shape leaped at me, struck me in the chest! I screamed.

It licked my face.

"Sadie. Damn you!" I could smell her old-dog breath as she settled down happily against my body.

There was a second door into my room, a door that was never used. It was just beside the head of my bed, and it led into the end of the upstairs corridor in the main house. My room was the connecting link between the house's upstairs and the apartment over the kennel. But Turner had given me the distinct impression, when I moved in, that kennel help did not wander about in the house uninvited. I'd set the small table with my portable television on it partially in front of that door, and had more or less forgotten the door's existence.

Now it was opened so hard and fast the TV almost hit the floor. Turner stood there in a maroon robe—one of those monk-style robes with the little hoods.

"Tabby? Are you all right?" His sightless eyes seemed to search for me.

"Yes. Sorry I screamed. It was just Sadie jumping on the bed."

"Good Lord," he said, disgusted. "I thought you were being murdered in here. You ought to be used to dogs jumping on you by now."

But he didn't seem angry. I switched on the light and sat up. "I know it. But Sadie doesn't usually come in here, she usually sleeps with Nancy. And I guess I had all this Ted business on my mind. It's making me a little jumpy."

He rubbed his eye with the heel of his hand and gave a dry sniff. "No reason for you to feel edgy. It's got nothing to do with you. You just tend to the dogs."

I ignored the curtly dismissive tone of his voice and the fact that he was backing out of the doorway, and said, "Turner? Do you think the threats are real? I mean, do you think Ted would be in danger if he judged?"

He hesitated, then said firmly, "Yes. I do. Those notes were the product of an unbalanced mind, and unbalanced minds are always dangerous. But it's not your concern, so go back to sleep."

He pulled the door shut. Thoughtfully I turned off the bed lamp and slid down to wrap my arms around Sadie. I found myself thankful for her company.

Saturday morning. Puppy Sweeptstakes day. I hurried through my kennel chores and finished them just in time for the nine o'clock start of the sweeps judging. The puppy classes were fun to watch, and the ringside areas were full of exhibitors in lawn chairs, sitting back in the benevolent morning sun to enjoy the show.

All the classes were large, twenty or more pups in each. There were dog and bitch classes, divided by colors and further divided by ages. Puppy dogs, six to nine months, black and white . . . and so on, through puppy bitches, twelve to eighteen months, liver and white. Then, later that afternoon when all the classes had been judged, the two top-placing pups in each class would compete for Best in Sweeps.

The judge was Lenora Greenblatt, who lived near Middlebury and just drove down for her judging assignment. She was an excellent judge but slightly antisocial, and avoided judges' dinners and any sort of gathering where exhibitors might be present. I admired her. That was the kind of judge I was going to be someday, not the Sally Tomas kind.

I watched three or four classes, then began to circle the area, looking for something that might need my attention. Turner, Ted, Louise, and the Tomases were sitting near the announcer's table, which was under the long tent, centered among the entrance gates to all four of the rings. Only one ring was in use today, but the Quinns were in the best possible spot to watch it. It would be shady under the tent all day.

I strolled past the trophy table and feasted my eyes. Yesterday's obedience trophies were replaced by the sweeps trophies, a huge silver coffee service for Best in Sweeps, engraved silver bowls in graduated sizes for the class winners and placements. Floral arrangements set off the silver beautifully.

At the corners of the trophy table and the announcer's table next to it were clusters of balloons, long, narrow balloons that had been cleverly twisted into the shapes of dogs. One of the Spaniel Club's members did balloon tying as a hobby. One night when the club meeting was at Quintessence, I'd watched, fascinated, as the man took a partially inflated balloon and, with a few deft twists, turned the long narrow balloon into a dachshund. He'd offered to make balloon dogs for the Specialty, and no one had had the heart to tell him that balloons would cheapen the decorations.

So here was a velvet-covered trophy table loaded with sterling and roses, with clusters of cheap balloons at the corners.

I went past the announcer's table where Mrs. Abernathy sat importantly beside her husband, who was doing the announcing for the show. He'd been on the stage decades ago, a vaudeville comedian when vaudeville was dying. He still had a surprisingly deep, mellifluous voice and he loved to use it, even though his main line today was "Clean-up boy to the ring, please."

I knelt behind Turner's chair and said, "I'm here."

"How do things look?" he asked without turning. "Trophy table all right?"

"Beautiful. Or it would be if we could get rid of those silly balloons."

"We can't do that without hurting Able's feelings," he said curtly. "When the show is over, you can give the balloons to kids or anybody who wants them, but we'll leave them up till then."

Sally Tomas sat beside Turner, giving him a play-by-play. "This one gaiting now is a Song and Dance puppy. Might mature out all right, awfully loose movement now, though. Topline like a trampoline, and he's got no front at all."

Phil Deitz was in the ring with a liver puppy waiting his turn to be gaited and posed. I saw his eyes search for Sally and connect, and I saw the loaded look he shot her. Loaded with what, I wasn't sure—complicity? promises? reminders? threats?

I glanced at Jim Tomas to see if he'd caught the look, but he was talking to Louise.

·2·

It was four o'clock before the silver coffee service was presented, with cheers and flashing cameras, to a teenage girl from Idaho. Her dog was an exuberant black-

and-white male, gangly and adolescent but full of quality. He was a popular choice. Everyone at ringside applauded full force, and the girl left the ring with tears streaming. Her parents had to carry the trophy and disentangle her from her dog.

I followed Turner and company toward the house for no particular reason. They didn't shoo me away, so I tagged along. It was too early to start evening kennel chores, and too hot to go to my room. Besides, I was curious about Ted. The last I'd heard, he was still stoutly declaring his intention to judge, but was also beginning to mention symptoms. A little stomach upset, a little headache . . . a flu bug that might conveniently prevent him from judging tomorrow?

Nancy met us near the house and told Turner she was going into town to the vet's if he hadn't already closed up. The puppies in the grooming-room pen were passing a little blood and mucous, probably just coccidiosis. She'd be back in an hour or so. Did he need anything from town?

He thought for a moment, then said she might pick up a half-dozen bottles of assorted booze for this evening, and a few bags of munchies.

She left, and I followed the three Quinns into the house. Ted and Louise ignored my presence. They settled in the living room, Ted to leaf through a copy of the *American Kennel Gazette,* Louise to help herself from the serving cart that doubled as a small bar.

Turner stood in the doorway to the living room, apparently lost in thought. His expression was one that usually meant he was about to tell me to do something, so I waited, watching him.

"Tabby."

I went over to him, close enough for him to feel my presence. His hand dropped on my shoulder and he said, in a low voice, "I want you to stay here and entertain Ted and Louise for a while. I'm having one of my headaches. I want to sleep it off before we go out to dinner."

Abruptly, he turned and went up the stairs to his room.

Entertain Ted and Louise? I mean, come on, boss. What entertaining did they need from me? Louise was already well into her second glass of whatever it was she was drinking, and Ted seemed engrossed in the magazine on his knee.

I went to the sofa and sat beside him. "Interesting article?" I asked.

He grunted without looking up.

Entertain the man, those were my orders. Make conversation, Tabby.

"So you're going to go ahead and judge tomorrow, huh?"

Well, I never claimed to be a tactful conversationalist.

He looked up at me then, his jowls quivering. Nerves or anger, I couldn't tell which. "My dear child," he said in a nasty pseudo-British accent, "if my health permits, I shall certainly—"

The phone rang.

I answered it at the ornate little desk in the corner of

85

the living room. "Quinn residence," I said, feeling like a maid in a play.

"Ted Quinn please. Police calling."

It wasn't Detective Holmes' voice though. In fact, the voice sounded odd, unnatural in some way, a deep male voice, but slightly muffled.

"Ted?" I said, holding out the phone. Then, quickly, I went through the hall into the kitchen. I made a "quiet" sound to Mrs. Jasper who was working at the sink. Cautiously, I picked up the wall phone and listened.

Ted was just saying hello.

"Ted Quinn," the voice said, "you got my notes? What are you going to do about them?"

My God, I thought. It's him. The threatener.

Ted gave a strangled sort of gasp and said, "Who is this?"

"You won't know until the end," the voice said.

"All right, then," Ted said quickly, "I won't judge. You win. I'll just tell them I'm sick."

The voice laughed, an ugly laugh. "Ted Quinn, the gutless wonder. I knew you'd fold. You're scared, aren't you, Ted? You're all white and shaky, like a jellyfish. You're sweating, aren't you? Have you thrown up yet, Ted? Or are you saving that for tomorrow, for when you pretend to be sick? Be a man, Ted Quinn. Call my bluff. Prove to your wife that you're more of a man than she gives you credit for."

Ted shouted, "What do you want from me? What do you want me to do? Who is this!"

The phone clicked, the threatening voice became a

dial tone. I hung up, too, and went back to the living room.

Ted was leaning heavily on the back of the desk chair, pasty-faced and sweating in the air-conditioned chill of the room.

"It was him," Ted gasped. Louise was already alerted, hearing only one end of the conversation, and had come to stand near Ted, her drink temporarily forgotten in her hand.

"What did he say? Who was it? Did you recognize the voice?"

"I was listening," I said.

Ted turned on me. "It was Turner, wasn't it?" he demanded. "He still hates me, Louise, I told you. He's never forgiven me, and now he's doing this to torment me. He wants to humiliate me, damn him."

I stopped replaying the voice in my head. It might or might not have been familiar, it was too muffled for me to be sure. And I'd been so absorbed in the words, I hadn't been trying to identify the voice, not at the time, anyhow.

"Did he threaten you again?" Louise demanded.

"Yes. Well, no, not actually." Ted looked suddenly puzzled. "I told him I wouldn't judge. I thought that would be the end of it. But then he started . . . taunting me. Calling me a coward." He glanced at me then, and I knew he hated me for hearing the taunts of cowardice. They were so evidently true.

"Well," I said suddenly, "it couldn't have been Turner who called. He's upstairs sleeping."

"How do you know that?" Louise asked sharply. "He could have called from an extension upstairs." Her voice dropped to a whisper, and all three of us turned to look toward the broad, curved stairway in the entry hall.

I shook my head. "If you call from one extension to another, it comes in on that other line." I pointed toward the row of buttons on the phone. "And the ring sounds different, too, more like a buzz. No, I'm sorry, this had to come from outside the house, and there's no way Turner could have snuck past us and gotten to a phone, not that fast."

Why had I said I was sorry? Did Ted so obviously want the caller to have been Turner? Apparently so, or I wouldn't have said that.

Immediately I began taking roll. The Tomases were outside somewhere, or had driven away . . . no, they had come by plane, they had no car here. But it was less than a quarter mile down the road to the Amoco station. And anyone at the show could have seen the Quinns walking up toward the house, could have presumed the houseguests would be resting before dinner.

Phil could have seen us all going into the house. Anyone could have. Sally, with her basso profundo voice . . .

Since no one else seemed to think of doing it, I called the police station and left a message for Detective Holmes, explaining what had happened. He called back a few minutes later, and I explained it again.

Ted took the phone from me and said, "Look here, what are you people planning to do to protect me tomorrow?"

I couldn't hear Holmes's answer, although I strained my ear.

"That's easy for you to say," Ted snapped. "I'm in a position here where I have to go through with it, or I'll never be able to hold up my head in the dog world again. At this point, even if I tell people I'm sick, who's going to believe me? I will have to judge, and you people will have to protect me, that's all there is to it."

He hung up and said to Louise, "The man's incompetent. He said he'd have a few plainclothesmen here tomorrow, but what good will that do? All these woods around here? All the motor homes, this house? There are any number of places a sniper with a telescopic sight could . . ." He shuddered.

Suddenly I laughed. "Well, at least you can't seriously think it's Turner, can you? I mean, come on. He gets around great, and does all kinds of wonderful things you wouldn't think a blind person could do. But . . . shooting someone? I mean, even up close he couldn't . . . well, maybe at point-blank range, but certainly not in the middle of a show ring."

They looked at me, and at each other.

"If he were threatening to poison you," I said more reasonably, "you might have something to worry about. But that bullet taped to the note, I mean, how clear can you be? And you couldn't poison somebody in the show ring."

We were all silent while we pictured the small judge's table that always sat just inside the rings to hold the ribbons, the judge's book, and a pitcher of water or a soft drink. Especially at summer shows, the judge's refreshment was always there on the table. No one else drank out of it, and anyone passing by might drop in something lethal.

But it was shooting that had been implied, by the note with the bullet on it. And shooting was beyond Turner Quinn's capabilities.

·3·

The Quinns and the Tomases drove off in the Cimarron around six, for dinner in town. Ted was at the wheel, making stilted jokes about being able to drive on the wrong side of the road. Just as though he hadn't been born and raised right here, I thought as I saw them off.

I'd finished evening chores by then and was lounging around near the kennel-office door as Ted backed the Cimarron out of the garage. Nancy was in the grooming room, popping tiny yellow tablets down puppies' throats to combat their coccidiosis. The show grounds were deserted except for a couple of women working their obedience dogs in the rings for practice. Through the trees I could see and hear and smell the steaks being grilled among the motor homes, the weary exhibitors stretched out on lawn chairs or wandering from rig to rig, visiting, cans of beer or soda in their hands.

I felt like going somewhere, joining someone, doing something. Supper upstairs in the apartment with Nancy just seemed too ordinary for a night like tonight. I was wound up like a cheap fiddle string, as my brother would say. The phone call that afternoon had shaken me, much more than the first note, or even the bullet. I had actually heard the voice of the . . . person . . . the threatener. That gave the threat a dimension of reality it hadn't quite carried before.

I'd hoped they might include me in the dinner trip, but Turner had felt his way into the car without seeking the sound of me. Silly hope, anyway. This was an adult dinner trip, to an expensive restaurant. Of course they weren't going to take the kennel girl.

Restlessly I wandered through the garage, through a service area, and into the kitchen. Mrs. Jasper was again or still at the sink, this time ripping up a head of lettuce.

"Can I help?" I asked, picking up a paring knife and a handful of lettuce.

"Not with that knife," she said sharply. "You cut lettuce with a carbon-steel knife blade and it'll turn the edges of the lettuce brown."

I set the knife down and cleared my throat apologetically. "Gee, we live and learn."

Mrs. Jasper was a comfortable sort of woman, barrel-shaped, with a sunken bosom and turkey-wattle jowls. She had a tooth missing, and never wore makeup of any kind. I preferred her sort of face to Louise's brittle painted-on features.

"Don't mind me, honey," Mrs. Jasper said. "All these houseguests are beginning to get to me, is all. I'm too old for this ruckus. Run down to the cellar and get me a pack of hamburger, would you? You can eat supper with me if you want."

I went back through the service area and down the basement steps to the oversized chest freezer that stood near the laundry equipment. The basement was used primarily for storing dog crates, old exercise pens, anything that didn't fit in anywhere else. It was cluttered but clean, hardly a "cellar."

I found the ground beef and took it back upstairs. "Isn't Mr. Jasper eating with us?" I asked as Mrs. J. put two of the frozen hamburger patties in the microwave to thaw.

"He won't be in till dark, I reckon. He wanted to get all the trash picked up before tomorrow."

We dug into the burgers and the huge bowl of tossed salad. When my mouth was free for talking purposes, I said, "Did you know Turner and Ted when they were young?"

"Oh, yeah. Well, we was all in school about the same time. Not that we ran in the same circles, nor nothing like that, but I knew them."

"Did Turner go to regular school?"

"Of course he did. What'd you expect?"

I shrugged. "Special school for the blind, I guess."

"Oh, Turner wasn't blind when we was kids. He had his accident, well, let me think. What was those boys, I guess around sixteen, seventeen when Turner had his accident."

I looked up in surprise. For some reason I'd always assumed Turner had been blind from birth. I couldn't think, now, where that impression had come from. "He was blinded by an accident? What kind?"

"Fell off a horse. Got a foot hung up in the stirrup, and the horse dragged him a ways. Hit his head on a cement cistern. Got some kind of damage to the optical nerve, the way I remember it."

"A horse?" Interesting.

"'Twas his brother's horse. Kinda spooky animal for anybody but Ted to ride, although it didn't cut up for Ted. Well, a horse can sense fear, don't you know. And Turner was always scared spitless of horses. He wasn't especially scared of other things, but horses just plain terrified that boy. The Quinns always had horses back then. Old Colonel Quinn, the boys' daddy, he had his hunters and so did the missus. Ted was a fair rider, did a little show riding although he wasn't much into the jumping, as I recall. But that Turner never wanted nothing to do with the horses. I can remember their daddy teasing that little boy, not the friendly kind of teasing, I don't mean. Taunting, more like. Making poor little Turner feel like a nothing, just because he didn't like to ride. And that Teddy, he was worse than their daddy, tormenting his brother with it."

"Hmm. I always thought twins were supposed to be close," I mused.

"Not those two. Seemed like they were always competing for their daddy's attention. I guess with them, being twins just made it worse. The competitiveness, don't you know."

She glopped us a couple of dishes of chocolate pudding, and I swirled up a spoonful thoughtfully.

93

"You don't think Turner is the one who's been threatening Ted, though, do you?" I asked.

"Oh, I wouldn't think so," she said firmly. "I can't see him doing anything that childish. And besides, how's a blind man going to shoot a gun? And why would he want to? Ted ain't doing him any harm now. He don't even live in this country. No, I'd say it's somebody that's showing a dog tomorrow. Or somebody that's got some strong reason for wanting that other lady to judge instead of Ted. That's the only thing that makes sense to me, not that any of it makes sense to me, come right down to it. I always did say those dog-show people don't have both oars in the water, most of them. Lord, the fuss they make over some animal's hind legs or how its tail is stuck on or how its ears hang. Only thing that's really important is if a dog'll protect you."

I thanked Mrs. Jasper for supper and wandered out again through the service area, through the kennel office, and out into the twilight. The grass looked blue in the fading light. There was just enough breeze to discourage mosquitoes. It was the kind of evening that made me tingle with unnamed expectations. Ordinarily.

Tonight my tingles were more like nervous anxiety. Tomorrow was the final day of the show. Tomorrow Ted would or would not judge, would or would not be . . . nah, it couldn't happen. This was real life. This was Katonah, this was Quintessence, this was a dog show, for heaven's sake. Not some stupid murder mystery on television. This was my own personal life, and nothing that exciting ever happened in it, despite tingles of unnamed expectations.

94

I found Nancy out back in one of the exercise yards, playing a puppy on a narrow show lead, like an angler playing a trout. The puppy had the lead in his mouth and was growling and thrashing his head in mock battle against the first restrictions of his young life.

"Well," I said as I sat down beside her on the ground, "what do you think's going to happen tomorow?"

Nancy snorted and shook the lead. "Nothing. I think old Ted will judge his classes; he's too worried about his image not to. And I think nothing will happen. I think the whole thing's a crock of dog puf."

Puf was her euphemism for what I cleaned out of the runs every day. Previously Utilized Food. One of the nicer ways of saying it, I thought.

"You know," I said thoughtfully, "the funny thing about that phone call this afternoon, I can't figure out why the guy didn't quit while he was ahead." I'd already told Nancy all about the call, during evening chores.

"I mean, Ted said he wouldn't judge. What more did the guy want?"

"Depends," Nancy said thoughtfully. "If this was a genuine threat, which I doubt, then it would depend on what the guy actually wanted."

I looked at her, puzzled. Then, slowly, I nodded. "You mean was he trying to scare Ted out of the show ring . . . or into it?"

Nancy turned her attention to the puppy, who had dropped the lead and was attacking her loafer tassels.

Looking at the phone conversation in that light, the man's attitude made some sense. It had sounded as though he was trying to shame Ted into going through with the judging. Which made no sense at all, since the same man had gone to such lengths to scare Ted out of judging.

Assuming it was the same man, of course.

Hours later, I was jerked awake by a tiny noise. Some instinct kept me frozen in position, curled on my side in bed, my face toward the back wall.

The noise was unmistakable. The door beside my bed, the door connecting my room with the upstairs hallway of the main house, was slowly opening.

Sunday, June 30

· 1 ·

I understood, then, the instinct that keeps rabbits frozen in the presence of an enemy. I could not have moved to save my life. After the waking shock I forced myself to go on breathing in a slow, regular, sleeper's rhythm.

The door bumped my television. I could hear the ping of the rabbit-ear antenna. "Not so loud," I prayed, "you'll wake me up."

His breath was loud in my room. A floorboard creaked beyond the foot of my bed. And then, beautiful sound, the opening of the other door, the fading away of the alien breath.

I sat up and stared first at one door, then the other. Both had been left an inch or two ajar, as though the intruder intended to come back this way.

Chilling thought.

I listened to his progress down the stairs, through the grooming room, through the door into the kennel office. Then another sound, the dialing of the telephone.

That was it, then, I thought, breathing loudly in relief. Not a murderer in the night, just someone from the house, shortcutting through my room to use the kennel phone, and not wanting to wake me up.

But why? Why not use the house phones? There were extensions everywhere. Unless they were out of order. . . . No, I heard behind me the distant ringing of the house phone.

I squinted at my watch. It was a cloudy night, not enough moonlight to illuminate the face. But the glow-in-the-dark hands of the alarm clock on the dresser appeared to be at around midnight.

Suddenly, a connection snapped into place in my mind. The kennel phone was separate from the house phones. A call from the kennel would look just like an outside call to someone answering in the house.

I knew, then.

Without stopping to think about what I was doing, I got out of bed and padded to the door. From the top of the stairs I could hear the low murmur of the voice, sending its threats to Ted.

Down the stairs I went in my bare feet, in my elongated nightshirt. I knew who was down there, and I wasn't afraid.

I should have been.

He hung up the phone when he heard me approach

and spun toward me. His expression should have warned me. It was intense to the point of blankness.

"Honestly," I said, "I never thought you'd do anything this—"

Incredible pain doubled me over, knocked me against the corner of the file cabinet. The hollow sound of a blow echoed in my head, then the ringing in my ears overwhelmed me, and I disappeared.

My first awareness was of discomfort. My legs seemed to be folded up hard against my chest. My skin hurt all over, and my neck felt broken, so tightly was my head forced downward toward my chest. The head itself was a bowl of pain.

I tried to stretch myself into a more comfortable position . . . and couldn't. Couldn't move my legs, or my arms, which seemed to be tied behind my back.

In my confusion I wasn't sure whether my eyes were closed, open, covered, or blinded. But gradually I began to perceive a limited field of vision, something that looked like fabric, folds of . . . oh, of course. It was my own chest, just inches away from my eyes. Wherever I was, it was almost totally dark. Only a tiny orange glow, from somewhere to my right, illuminated my situation.

Gradually my head cleared of its fogginess, although the pain stayed and grew. I was tied up, somewhere, and my mouth was gagged. It was tied open, with something thick and soft jammed into it and knotted behind my head.

With that realization came an overwhelming need to

swallow, to breathe. I seemed to be drowning in my own saliva, unable to work my tongue or my throat.

It's just panic, I told myself, and in a little while the feeling subsided and I was able to breathe almost normally.

With clearer awareness came sharper pain. I was lying on my side, my knees forced up hard against my chest, my forehead almost touching my bare kneecaps. Behind me, my wrists were tied with something that felt like narrow bands of hard fabric. Actually I was lying at an angle, mostly on my side but partially on my back, my knees pointing upward at a slight angle.

Pressing into my skin on all sides were what felt like walls of some sort of metal mesh. I could feel lines of something like thick wire forming inch-wide squares against my flesh. Soles of my feet, kneecaps, back and shoulders and lower hip, all pressed painfully against the mesh, and the areas that bore the weight of my body were pressing so painfully that I would have cried if there hadn't been worse things to worry about.

Through my panic-thoughts began to run threads of memory. Someone had come through my room in the night, and stupidly I'd followed. What then? The memory was blurred, but I forced myself through it. Down the stairs, into the kennel office, and then . . .

I hadn't seen him clearly. The office was black. But I knew who he was, and he knew I was there. The darkness that hampered me gave him the advantage. He was accustomed to radaring in on small sounds of breath and movement.

The sharp stab of pain in my stomach? His cane. I'd seen the blur of white motion coming at me, but disbelief slowed my reactions. I'd folded around the agony of the sharp cane driven into my stomach. I'd fallen against something. Desk? File cabinet. The fall knocked me out, or Turner did, I wasn't sure, and it didn't make much difference now.

He'd carried or dragged me somewhere. . . .

How long ago? I had no way of knowing. It was still night, unless I was somewhere without windows.

I tried to clear my thoughts, to use my senses to orient myself. The atmosphere seemed to be cool, faintly damp. I could smell, beyond the subtle familiarity of my own skin and nightshirt, something like stone or concrete, something else with a perfumy fragrance, and a trace of dog.

The tiny orange glow. What could that be?

Sounds? A faint hum, the sort of motor noise that is always in the background, an appliance motor. Kitchen appliance? No, he wouldn't have left me in the kitchen.

A sudden loud swoosh terrified me.

When my heart quit pounding in my ears, the swoosh had settled into a rhythmic chugging sound. It was familiar. I knew that sound. It was . . .

Oh, of course. A water softener, set to recharge itself during the night.

Awareness came flooding in on me then. I was in the basement. The concrete floor was just under my face, and the perfumy fragrance came from the floral scent of the fabric softener strips Mrs. Jasper used in the dryer.

I'd teased her about using them for the kennel laundry. The tiny orange glow, then, would be the light on the front of the freezer, indicating that it was running.

And my cage was just that. It was, it had to be, one of the Kennel-Aire dog crates Nancy had relegated to the basement. Turner knew they were down here. He'd dragged me through the garage and down the basement stairs, and tied me and gagged me so I couldn't yell, and thrown me into a dog crate.

Outrage filled me. How could he do something like that, I fumed. How could he handle me that way? We were friends. I thought we were friends. I liked him, and he knew it and seemed to like to have me around. I'd fought the possibility that it was he who was threatening Ted. I'd fought that possibility even when the logic was compelling.

I had not *wanted* Turner to be the kind of man who would do something this bizarre.

I turned away from that hurtful thought, to more practical problems. How was I going to get out of here?

I twisted my hands, worked my fingers, found nothing that I could do with them. The cramping in my legs and neck was growing unbearable, and when I focused my attention on my physical position, I became unable to draw more than quick, shallow breaths. There seemed to be no room for my lungs.

Get out of the crate, then, I told myself. If I could just get out of the crate, get free in the basement, I could find some way to rid myself of the gag and the wrist-tie.

I forced myself to remember everything I could about

the Kennel-Aire crates. They were made of extremely sturdy wire mesh, with a dog-sized door in the end panel. The door would be too small, I knew. I'd tried to crawl into a crate once, to clean it after a show trip, and could only get my head and one arm through the door. I'd had to clean it by opening the lid.

The Kennel-Aires were made to fold down flat, for shipping or storage. The top of the crate opened upward, then the side pulled loose, and the whole thing collapsed into a giant cross shape, with the top, sides, and bottom all laid out in a continuous strip, the front and back panels hinged to fold up into position.

So all I had to do was to unlatch the roof of the crate and push it upward, and the whole thing would fall away.

But the unlatching was tricky. I remembered fiddling with it for several minutes, that day, before Nancy came to show me how to do it. Simple, when you knew how.

Simple, from the outside.

From my position, almost impossible.

·2·

My hopes sank as I formed mental pictures of the crate's fastening system. The top of the crate had an inch of overlap on three sides, fitting down over the front, back, and one side panel, like a box lid. It was hinged to the other side panel.

This inch of overlap was held in place against the side panel by a pair of simple D-shaped wire tabs sticking out from the side panel, an inch down from the top. Another pair of D-shaped wire tabs dropped down from the top, falling just behind the edge of the side panel.

To assemble the crate, you just had to lay it out in its flat cross-shape, raise the front and back panels into position, raise the left side panel and fit it against the front and back panels, then raise the right side and the top, tamp them into snug position against the front and back, and secure the top in place. To do that, you'd flip up the two D-tabs on the top panel, drop the top into place, and push gently against the side panel to force the side D-tabs inward. Then, tap the top down into position, release the side panel, and its D-tabs would then protrude through the mesh of the top panel's overlap. Drop the two D-tabs on top down into their position, and they would prevent the sides from being pushed inward far enough to release the top.

It was an excellent, functional design, slick as goose-grease for someone standing outside the crate.

My eyes were adjusted to the dark now, and I could see, barely, the D-tab in the crate top, the one farthest from my face. The other was too close, somewhere just above my forehead. I was going to have to push up both of those D-tabs, then pull in the side panel until its D-tabs were clear of the overlap. Then, simply push up on the top, and I'd be free.

I tried to maneuver my foot toward the tab, but it wouldn't go. My knee was already against my chest, and my foot simply couldn't reach the tab. I tried for several minutes, tried shifting myself upward, tried twisting farther over onto my back. I still couldn't reach the tab.

If I had my hands, it would be so simple. Again I twisted my wrists. The edges of their binding cut into my skin. Hopelessly, I wept.

Then I rested and tried to think clearly. I became aware that I was seeing farther now, and it wasn't just night vision. Gray morning light was coming in through the small, high basement window over the washer and dryer.

Mrs. Jasper would come down to get something out of the freezer for breakfast. Someone would come down, for something. Maybe.

Or maybe not. Breakfast stuff wasn't in the freezer. Breakfast would be eggs, toast, maybe cinnamon buns, nothing that wasn't already in the kitchen. And it was Sunday morning, with a big dog show going on outside. Neither Nancy nor Mrs. Jasper was likely to come down here this morning.

And this afternoon, Ted Quinn would do his judging, and Turner Quinn would do . . . whatever it was he intended to do.

As I lay exhausted and hurting, I realized that what we'd all tended to consider a questionable threat at most was in fact a very serious threat. Turner wouldn't have gone to such extremes to keep me out of the way if he wasn't planning something more than just scaring Ted. In some way I couldn't imagine, Turner was going to kill his brother in a few hours, not five hundred yards from where I lay. And I had to be kept here until it was finished.

I realized then how single-minded, how obsessive, Turner was about this. Surely he knew that I'd be found here, alive and able to talk, within a day or so at most. He might tell Nancy some story to explain my absence from morning kennel chores, and later in the day the confusion of the final day of judging would cover my absence. Everyone who had time to think about me at all would simply assume I was somewhere else at the moment.

Turner's fixation on Ted must have been so strong that he couldn't see past the killing to the consequences. But why? Turner had been living what seemed to be a happy life, until Ted came. His blindness was an inconvenience he'd learned to live around, building an extremely profitable business with his inventive mind and his sharp business skills. He'd never married, but in my opinion that had nothing to do with his blindness or with Ted. He was simply a very self-centered man who wanted absolute control of his household and who had probably never felt a strong need for a wife. He'd had women friends when he wanted them according to Nancy, but didn't seem to need them, particularly, and had always broken from them when they began hinting about marriage.

He loved his dogs, or at least he loved the winning that his dogs did. He loved his home, his wardrobe, his music, his work until he'd retired.

Of course I hadn't known him before his retirement two years ago, but now I recalled a conversation Nancy and I had had once, when we were on the subject of Turner. "He used to be a lot happier," she'd said. "He shouldn't have retired so young. He has too much mental energy. He gets moody so often now, and he wasn't that way when he had his company to run. I think his blindness depresses him more now, too. He's got more time to think about it, I suppose."

I tried to imagine myself in Turner's place. He'd spent most of his life building up his business, using his inventiveness to design better and better medical instruments, making more and more money. Then, maybe to prove his success, he retired in his midforties, still a mental athlete but with no more challenges.

Did he begin to resurrect old hates then? His brother was, in a way, responsible for Turner's blindness, if I understood Mrs. Jasper's story correctly. A lifelong contest between the brothers, to prove themselves in their father's eyes. Turner brave at some things but with an inborn fear of horses; Ted timid about some things, but not of his horse, an animal too tricky for strange riders to handle. A hated brother's goading, a defiant ride, a fall, and a life of blindness.

Could thoughts like these, simmering in Turner's idled mind, have produced some bizarre plan to avenge his blindness on Ted?

Could Turner have been the moving force behind the invitation to judge the National Specialty? Was there a plan, carefully worked out, to publicly humiliate Ted by forcing him to display cowardice before the dog-show world? Or was the plan to kill Ted?

But if that were the case, then why the threats aimed at discouraging Ted from judging?

I didn't understand. And I hurt.

My legs were cramping painfully. My shoulder was asleep under me, so the pain of wire mesh pressing against unpadded shoulder bones had diminished, but the wire embedded in my thigh and elbow and knees more than made up for the deadened shoulder.

Again I struggled to reach the D-tab. By shifting farther onto my back, and by forcing my left leg hard up against my chest, I was finally able to twist my left ankle inward and press my big toe against the crate top, just three mesh-square inches away from the tab.

Grunting, gasping for breath, rolling my eyes upward as hard as I could in order to see where my foot was going, I managed to move the toe over one more square. Then one more.

I could feel the edge of the tab, but I couldn't move any closer toward it. The other toes on that foot had popped upward through the mesh of the crate top and halted my progress.

Cursing, I slid the foot cautiously downward until the toes were bent back by the next line of mesh. Then sideways again, and the toe was under the tab.

"Please," I prayed, and moved my toe. The tab lifted, hesitated, fell back into place.

"Damn you," I thought, and kicked with all the power in my big toe. The D-tab rose—and stayed!

There was still the other top tab, the one above my head. Impossible to reach with a foot. I forced myself downward an inch, hoping to be able to bend my head back far enough to see the tab.

Gradually, a fraction at a time, I shoved my head back, back hard against the mesh behind it, so hard I wanted to cry from the pain in my scalp. One row of crate-top wire came into view, then another and another, but still no tab.

I couldn't understand it. It shouldn't be this far back, I thought. It should be right about . . .

And then I saw it. It had been hidden from sight because it was already standing upright. Turner had missed it when he shut me in.

The tabs were out of the way! Now all I had to do was to pull the side panel inward until its tabs were clear of the overlap. Then, push up on the top and I'd be out.

Just pull the side panel inward half an inch. So simple.

But I couldn't do it.

·3·

There was simply no way to pull inward the wire wall against which my shoulder and hip were jammed. I had nothing to grab with, only one bare foot that didn't reach that far. And if I had been able to grasp the wire and pull it toward me, it would have taken strength and leverage to get it far enough inward to clear the catch tabs.

I lay in my cramped and folded position through the

endless hours of the morning, intermittently struggling, swearing silently, and lying back to think. My jaw ached unbearably from the gag.

I don't know how long I'd been looking at the laundry table before I saw its possibilities. If I couldn't pull the crate panel inward, possibly something could push it.

To my right, just in the corner of my vision, stood an elderly card table on which Mrs. Jasper sorted and folded laundry. The table itself was too flimsy to be of help, but the large plastic jug of liquid detergent sitting on the table . . . if the jug were full enough to be heavy, and if I could move the crate over there, and roll the damned thing over onto its side. . . .

I whipped my body sideways. The crate scooted the merest fraction of an inch toward the table. I whipped again, clenching against the pinching of my flesh between basement floor and shifting wire mesh.

The distance was about four feet from crate to table. It took probably more than two hours of thrashing, resting, gritting, and thrashing again, to scoot the crate those four feet.

As the table grew closer, I flung my knees and shoulders hard to the left. The crate rocked. I tried again, giving it more than I had to give. The crate rocked, teetered, and fell onto its side. I wept with relief, both physical and mental.

The laundry table was now behind my back, and I was lying more or less on my left side. The crate top had become its side, the side panel to which the top was latched had become the topmost surface.

It was harder in this position to move the crate table-ward, because I'd lost the power of my swinging knees. I battered backward with my head and shoved with my willpower.

Suddenly I felt the crate bump against the flimsy folding leg of the table. Here goes nothing, I breathed, and rocked one more time.

The table toppled onto the crate, and the detergent jug rolled beautifully downward. It hit the crate, springing the panel downward, and popping open the top.

My joy was so great that I hardly felt the cold, thick, blue liquid pouring over me.

Wriggling spastically, I got my legs free. They refused to straighten at first, then did so with the tingle of returning circulation, followed by breath-taking stabs of muscle cramps.

I rolled the rest of the way out and hunched on my knees for several minutes until my legs were able to hold me up. As desperate as I was to get free from the wrist ties and the gag, I decided it was more important to get upstairs, outdoors, anyplace where someone could help me.

I had to lean against the stair railing all the way up, for fear my legs would buckle under me. The door at the top was closed. Cautiously I pivoted my body, praying I wouldn't fall down the stairs. My hands couldn't find the knob. It was too high or too low or something.

Weakly, furiously, I banged my head against the door. I banged and banged, knowing it might well be Turner who found me.

But when at last the door opened, it was Nancy's arms I toppled into.

"My God," was all she could say.

It had been a lifetime since I'd given a thought to what I looked like, but I must have been a picture by then. Thigh-length cotton shirt with a picture of Snoopy astride his doghouse, shooting at the Red Baron. Hair literally on end. Blood, both dried and oozing, in my hair and on my back and legs, where my skin had been pinched and scraped between mesh and concrete. Bare feet, hands tied, mouth gagged, eyes wild, and the whole thing frosted over with Liquid Blue Cheer.

It took Nancy a full minute to absorb the sight and to get to work on the knotted gag. Bless her, she knew where the worst spot was. When the pressure was gone from my mouth, I tried to say something, but jaws and tongue weren't working yet.

I stared at the gag. It was one of Turner's socks. Unwashed. I had just spent twelve hours with a dirty sock in my mouth. My stomach lurched.

Nancy was working furiously behind my back. I couldn't feel the ties when they came off, my hands were so numb. She reached around in front of me and dangled the tie. It was a brown nylon show lead, half an inch wide, impossible to break.

"Can you talk yet?" Nancy asked.

I wanted to collapse into her arms and be cosseted and mothered and petted and nursed back to health. But in the distance I heard Mr. Abernathy's voice on the P.A. system. The show was going on.

112

I moved my jaw, my tongue. "Ted?" I said.

Nancy looked blank. Then she gave her head a small shake and said, "He's in the ring. They're doing Best in Show. I just came back for a minute to check on the pups and heard you banging."

We were in the service area between kitchen and garage. "Come on," I croaked. "Ted. Turner."

I started out through the door, across the lawn toward the show rings. Nancy ran after me, yelling, "You can't go out there looking like that."

Two of the rings had been combined to make one huge show ring, for this, the high point of the show season for springer spaniel people. The day was perfect, clear and sunny with enough breeze to make ringside sitting pleasant. Watchers were six-deep around the ring, in lawn chairs, on the ground, and standing.

If people turned to stare at me, and I'm sure they must have, I wasn't aware of it then. I darted behind and among the watchers, straining to find Turner.

Within the ring, sixty of the finest springer champions in the country stood posed like cardboard statues, black and white, liver and white, their ears and leg feathering blowing gently in the breeze. The grass was vivid green. Floral arrangements stood in the center of the ring at the base of the low platform where the winner would pose for photographs.

With his back to me, Ted Quinn moved down the line of dogs. He wore a pale gray seersucker suit and a natty British cap. At first glance he appeared to be judging his class as usual. But even thirty yards away I could see the jerkiness of his movements. He bent to check a dog's testicles and almost overbalanced. The dog's handler had to catch him and steady him.

Then I saw Turner. He was standing almost directly in front of me, at the ring's edge. We were both under the shade of the center tent. Turner stood in the narrow space between the trophy table with its balloons and the table at which Mr. Abernathy sat behind the loudspeaker's microphone.

As I watched, Turner reached a casual hand toward the balloons. His fingers separated one balloon string from the others and pulled it toward him. The green dog-shaped balloon passed across Turner's body and stopped just below the microphone, held there by Turner's palm against the edge of the table.

Confused, I watched as Turner shifted a lighted cigarette into the hand just under the balloon.

But Turner did not smoke.

Too late, I lunged forward, shouting his name.

His hand jerked upward. The cigarette touched the balloon.

The explosion was magnified by the mike and sent echoing out across the show ring.

Ted Quinn jerked. Eyes staring, hands clutching at his chest, he fell.

Afterword

I hadn't even known Turner's mother was alive. She came up from Florida in time for the funeral and stayed on in the house through the long months of waiting for Turner's trial.

Heart attack, they'd called it, when the paramedics came to take Ted from the show ring. He was alive then, but died later that night in the Katonah hospital.

Dog shows are wondrous things. They are never called because of weather. Tornadoes or hurricanes might temporarily dislodge dog shows, but they cannot stop them. The Best of Breed class was excused temporarily, until the ambulance was out of sight. Then the sixty handlers were called from their shady waiting places and ushered back into the ring for the completion of the judging.

Sally Tomas awarded Best in Show honors to Ch. Redstone's Grampa Jones, owned by Jack and Mary Pnobscot, handled by Phil Deitz.

Detective Holmes and three of his men materialized from the shadows when it was too late and escorted Turner into the house for questioning. They had been prowling the woods and crowds looking for a gun. They hadn't thought of a dog-shaped balloon and a lit cigarette as potential murder weapons.

And those things alone wouldn't have done it, not without the terror, the expectation of gunfire, that Turner had planted in his brother's mind with notes and phone calls.

There was another weapon, too. Turner's mother explained to Holmes that the boys' father had died of a heart attack in his early forties. Turner himself had irregularities, a minor heart murmur. Holmes found that out from Turner's doctor. Given the family medical background and the fact that Ted was Turner's twin, the odds were that Ted, too, carried an imperfect heart. And Ted was overweight and flabby.

Turner sat with placid dignity through the questioning in the living room. I was there, cleaned up and dressed and bandaged, to explain what Turner had done to me.

At one point Turner had said to me, "I didn't mean for you to be hurt, Tabby. I'm glad you got out all right."

His face was calm, almost smiling. It gave me chills.

"Why did you come through my room?" I demanded. Detective Holmes followed our exchange closely.

116

"Ted and Louise were downstairs in the living room," Turner explained. "I couldn't very well go out past them and around to the kennel, could I?"

His coolness was unnerving. He had no intention of doing his brother serious harm, he explained over and over, as though Holmes were not bright. He only intended to pay Ted back, in fright and public humiliation, for the accident that had cost him his sight.

"Ted knew I was afraid of that horse," he said in a voice that was suddenly boyish and uncertain. "He wanted me to look bad in front of Daddy. He was always doing that to me. Now we're even."

Holmes just shook his head, as though he had now heard everything.

The motor homes drove away one by one, and Foley's crew folded away the tenting and the show rings.

The show was over.

When the police released Ted's body, Louise flew back to London with it, for funeral services there. Turner's mother settled into the house as a temporary measure, and Turner went into the county jail, pending his hearing and trial. I felt a pang of sorrow for him. He'd miss his beautiful clothes, his good food, his clean, ordered existence.

Nancy and I went on taking care of the dogs. Eventually Mrs. Quinn made arrangements to sell her condo in Fort Lauderdale and settled into the house permanently. She was a quiet, small woman who seemed overwhelmed

whelmed at first by the house, although she must have been its mistress for many years before her husband died. I liked her. She came out to the kennel often, not to check on our work but just to stroke a dog and talk to Nancy or me.

Turner Quinn did not come to trial. Four months after Ted's death, Turner's own heart failed and he died in his cell. I cried when I heard about it. And I wondered if perhaps the brothers were tied more firmly to each other than anyone had realized.